"I put in that safe house request. There's a place near here, and a marshal's checking it out now."

Jordan nodded and sipped her coffee, but Egan noticed that wasn't exactly a happy look she was sporting. "You don't think the safe house is a good idea?" But he didn't wait for her to answer. "Surely you don't want to spend another night in here with me."

It was a simple comment, definitely nothing sexual, but it didn't get a simple response. Jordan's gaze came to his, and he saw the heat again. Maybe because of the whole "spending the night together" thing. They hadn't done that in years, but the last time had been when they were still lovers. And he darn sure hadn't slept in a chair back then. He'd been in bed with her.

LAWMAN WITH A CAUSE

USA TODAY Bestselling Author
DELORES FOSSEN

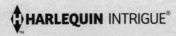
HARLEQUIN INTRIGUE®

Recycling programs
for this product may
not exist in your area.

ISBN-13: 978-1-335-64057-4

Lawman with a Cause

Copyright © 2018 by Delores Fossen

Printed in U.S.A.

www.Harlequin.com

Delores Fossen, a *USA TODAY* bestselling author, has sold over seventy-five novels, with millions of copies of her books in print worldwide. She's received a Booksellers' Best Award and an RT Reviewers' Choice Best Book Award. She was also a finalist for a prestigious RITA® Award. You can contact the author through her website at www.deloresfossen.com.

Books by Delores Fossen

Harlequin Intrigue

The Lawmen of McCall Canyon

Cowboy Above the Law
Finger on the Trigger
Lawman with a Cause

Blue River Ranch

Always a Lawman
Gunfire on the Ranch
Lawman from Her Past
Roughshod Justice

**The Lawmen of
Silver Creek Ranch**

Grayson
Dade
Nate
Kade
Gage
Mason
Josh
Sawyer
Landon
Holden

HQN Books

A Wrangler's Creek Novel

Lone Star Cowboy
(ebook novella)
Those Texas Nights
One Good Cowboy
(ebook novella)
No Getting Over a Cowboy
Just Like a Cowboy
(ebook novella)
Branded as Trouble
Cowboy Dreaming
(ebook novella)
Texas-Sized Trouble
Cowboy Heartbreaker
(ebook novella)
Lone Star Blues
Cowboy Blues
(ebook novella)
The Last Rodeo

A Coldwater Texas Novel

Lone Star Christmas

Visit the Author Profile page at Harlequin.com.

CAST OF CHARACTERS

Sheriff Egan McCall—Two years ago he lost his fiancée, Shanna, to a gunman's bullet, but now someone is murdering the people who received Shanna's organs. Egan vows to protect the remaining recipients, even if that puts him on a collision course with both his old flame and the killer.

Jordan Gentry—A former cop who not only got one of Shanna's organs but was also Egan's high school sweetheart. Egan blames her in part for Shanna's death, but as the killer targets them, Egan and she must put their pasts aside to stay alive.

Detective Christian Abrams—Jordan and he now work together reviewing death penalty convictions to make sure there were no irregularities in the trials, but Christian might have a secret that's putting both Egan and Jordan in danger.

Tori Judd—A lawyer who also got one of Shanna's organs. Now the killer is after her.

Drew Paxton—The man who's on death row for killing Shanna. Is he somehow responsible for the new murders?

Kirk Paxton—Drew's brother. He despises Egan and Jordan because he feels they should have done more to stop Drew from killing Shanna, and he could be out for revenge.

Leeroy Sullivan—Shanna's father, who's still grief-stricken over his daughter's death. He might be connected to the murders of the organ recipients.

Chapter One

The moment he took the turn to his ranch, Sheriff Egan McCall spotted the emergency lights flashing on the vehicle just ahead. He groaned. Then he cursed.

Even in the darkness, he recognized the old white truck. It was parked on the shoulder of the narrow country road, and the driver was definitely someone he didn't want to see tonight. Or any other night for that matter.

Jordan Gentry.

Egan had only wanted to get home and get some sleep since he'd just pulled a twelve-hour shift and was bone tired. But sleeping anytime soon likely wasn't going to happen if he had to deal with Jordan first.

What the heck was she doing out here anyway?

The only place on this road was the Mc-

Call Ranch, which meant Jordan had probably been going there to see him. That couldn't be right, though. Jordan hadn't spoken a word to him in two years, and Egan wanted it to stay that way.

He pulled to a stop behind her truck and dragged in a deep breath that he hoped would steel him up. He hated, too, that steeling up was even required when it came to Jordan. Once, she'd been his high school sweetheart, but that felt like a lifetime ago. Now she was just part of the nightmarish memories that he still hadn't figured out a way to forget.

Egan got out, walking on the gravel shoulder to the driver's side. Since the engine wasn't running, he looked inside, expecting to see Jordan behind the wheel ready to complain about not being able to get her truck started. But both the headlights and emergency lights were on, so this couldn't be about a dead battery. Maybe she was having engine trouble.

Jordan wasn't there, though, in the cab of the truck. No one was. But Egan spotted something he definitely hadn't wanted to see.

Blood.

It was on the seat. So were chunks of safety

glass. The passenger-side window was completely shattered.

Egan turned around so he could see if Jordan was nearby. Maybe she'd tried to avoid running into an animal or something and had hit her head. Of course, that didn't explain the broken window.

"Jordan?" he called out.

No response. There were deep ditches next to her truck and a fence just beyond that. But Egan didn't see her.

He took out his phone, using it as a flashlight, and spotted more blood on the ground. Not a huge amount, but even a few drops were enough to concern him. He needed to call for an ambulance.

However, the sound stopped him from doing that.

It was a soft rustling noise at the front end of the truck. Egan drew his gun, and he stepped closer.

Jordan.

She was sitting on the ground, her back against the front fender of her truck, and she had her gun gripped in her right hand, her phone in her left. She turned, and thanks to the truck headlights, he had no trouble seeing the source of the blood. It was on the top of her shoulder, just to the side of her blond hair, and it was running down the sleeve of her shirt.

"Are you here to finish me off?" she asked.

Obviously, she was dazed and didn't know what she was saying. Egan made that call to get an ambulance out there.

"What happened?" He went closer, peeling off his own shirt so he could wipe away some of the blood and see just how badly she was hurt.

"You" was all she said. She laughed. It was hoarse and weak, and it definitely wasn't from humor. "I knew you hated me, but I never thought in a million years you'd try to kill me."

Yeah, she was definitely talking crazy. Egan had a look at her wound and saw the gash on her shoulder. He eased her hair aside so he could see if there were other injuries, and she also had a bump on her head. She'd need stitches and might even have a concussion.

"What happened?" Egan repeated.

"You tried to kill me," she said without hesitation.

Even though Jordan was hurt, it was still hard to keep the scowl off his face. He tapped his sheriff's badge in case she'd forgotten that he was the law around here and not prone to murder attempts. "And why would I do that?"

There were tears in her pale green eyes when Jordan looked up at him. "Shanna."

Everything inside Egan went still.

Shanna Sullivan. His late fiancée. Shanna was also the reason Jordan was no longer someone he wanted to see. Even now after nearly two years, he still felt the ache. It ate away at him, and sometimes, like now, the ache felt just as fresh as it had when Shanna had died less than an hour after a man had shot her.

He leaned in, sniffed Jordan's breath to make sure she hadn't been drinking. She hadn't been. "Focus," he demanded. "I didn't try to kill you and neither did Shanna. She's dead. So, what the hell happened here?"

She touched her fingers to her head and looked at the blood that was on the sleeve of her shirt. "I...uh, was driving to your place to talk to you, and someone started to pass me. At least I thought that's what he was doing, but then he shot me. Someone driving a blue pickup identical to yours."

Egan pulled back his shoulders. He hoped like the devil that none of that was true. He definitely didn't want someone firing shots into a vehicle. Especially someone who might be posing as him. But then he reminded himself that Jordan hadn't made much sense with anything else she'd said.

He had another look at that gash on her shoulder. It was possibly a deep graze from a bullet. *Possibly.* But it could have also happened if she'd hit her head and shoulder on the steering wheel. Of course, her accusation would mesh with the broken window. Not with anything else, though.

"After he shot me, my truck stalled. I couldn't get it started," she continued a moment later. "So, I got out to try to fix it. That's when I passed out and landed here on the ground."

Egan didn't bother to tell her it'd been stupid to try to do engine repairs while injured. "You should have called nine-one-one."

Despite being dazed, she managed to give him a flat look. "Right. Call the local cops when I thought it was a local cop who shot me. I called someone from San Antonio PD instead."

He supposed that wasn't really a surprise about her not wanting to alert the locals. After all, Jordan lived in San Antonio, where she'd once been a cop. She almost certainly still had friends on the force there. But it was a long drive, nearly an hour, from San Antonio to McCall Canyon, and it'd likely be a while before her friend made it out here.

"And your cop friend in San Antonio didn't convince you to call me?" Egan asked.

"No." Again, she didn't hesitate. "Not after everything that's happened."

She was talking about Shanna now. Specifically, Shanna's murder. But Egan had no intention of getting into that with Jordan tonight.

"Come on," he said, helping her to her feet. In case she was still thinking he would try to kill her, he took her gun and put it in the back waistband of his jeans. "We can wait in my truck until the ambulance gets here." Which should be in about only twenty minutes or so.

If Jordan was right about having been shot, Egan didn't want them to be out in the open in case the shooter returned. Of course, he doubted that would happen. The bullet—if it was indeed a bullet—had probably come from someone out hunting.

"Hold my shirt against your shoulder to slow down the bleeding," Egan instructed.

Jordan went stiff when he tried to get her moving, and she looked at him as if debating if she could trust him.

Egan cursed again. "I don't know what you think happened here, but I didn't shoot you. I have no reason to kill you."

"Yes, you do." She lifted the side of her top to show him something he didn't need to see. The scar. The one from her surgery two years ago.

"So?" he snapped. "Did you think I'd forgotten you had a kidney transplant?" It wasn't a question because there was no way he could have not remembered that. After all, the donor kidney had come from Shanna.

Hell. More memories came. Jordan had been shot that day, too. The bullet had gone through her side and damaged both her kidneys. It'd been somewhat of a miracle that Shanna had been a match. Of course, that miracle came with a huge price tag since Shanna was dead.

"No. I didn't think you'd forgotten at all." She swallowed hard. "In fact, that's why I thought you wanted me dead."

"You're not making sense." He hooked his arm around her waist and forced her to get moving again.

He helped her into his truck, and she winced when she pressed his shirt against her head. Egan considered just driving her to the hospital, but the ambulance could arrive soon, and he could hand her off to the medics while staying behind to have a look at her vehicle. Specifically, that window. He wanted to see if the damage had indeed been caused by a bullet, and if so, then he could call out a CSI team.

"Yes, I am making sense," Jordan snarled. "Two of the recipients are already dead, and I think I'm next."

"Recipients?" he questioned.

She looked up at him. "You hadn't heard?"

No. But Egan was 1,000 percent sure he wasn't going to like what Jordan was about to say next.

"Breanna Culver, who got Shanna's liver. Cordell Minter, who got one of her lungs.

They're both dead. Murdered." Jordan's last word didn't have much sound. It was mostly breath.

Hell. If that was true…well, Egan didn't want to go there just yet. "It could be a co-incidence." Though it would be an eerie one. "You're positive they were murdered?" he challenged.

Jordan's forehead bunched up. "Yes. Their organs were…missing. The organs they got from Shanna."

Egan felt as if someone had punched him. "If that's true, why didn't someone tell me?"

"Because I only made the connection today. I knew the names of the recipients. I got them because, well, I don't know why exactly. Maybe I wanted to know who else was alive because of Shanna. I thought it would give me some peace."

Egan's mind was reeling, but he wanted to tell her that she didn't deserve peace. Neither of them did. "You're positive about those two people? Positive they were murdered and their organs taken?"

She nodded and motioned to her head. "And now this. Someone shot me."

No way could he just accept all of this just yet. "Your injury could have been a prank gone wrong. Or a hunter. It could have even been caused by a rock going through the window. A rock that maybe a passing truck kicked up from the road."

Her expression let him know she wasn't buying any of this. "What about the break-in at my house?"

He was clueless about that, too, but then he hadn't kept up with Jordan.

"I was supposed to be home," she continued. "But I'd left only about five minutes before to go into San Antonio to meet one of my old criminal informants. I wanted to ask him about the other two deaths. Anyway, while I was gone, someone broke in and set fire to the place."

Again, that didn't mean anyone was trying to murder her—though the "coincidences" were stacking up.

"That means there are only three of us left," Jordan added a moment later. "Tori Judd, Irene Adair. And me."

Egan hadn't known the names of the people who'd gotten Shanna's organs. He hadn't wanted to know. But was it possible someone was going after these people. And if so, why?

One name instantly came to mind. Drew Paxton.

The man who'd put a lethal bullet in Shanna. A bullet that Drew had fired during a botched hostage situation that had killed Shanna.

"Drew Paxton is in jail on death row," Egan heard himself mumble.

Jordan made a sound of agreement even though Egan hadn't been talking to her. "And he hasn't had any unusual visitors. You know, the kind of visitors he could have hired to kill people."

Egan was well aware of that because while he hadn't kept tabs on Jordan, he had done just that with Drew. It wasn't a morbid curiosity, either. Shanna had been Drew's parole officer, and the snake had developed a fixation on her. So much so that he'd broken into Shanna's house in San Antonio and taken her hostage.

Jordan had been one of the responding officers. A hostage negotiator. And she'd failed big-time. So had Egan. Because he hadn't been able to save Shanna, and he'd lost the woman he loved.

"I ruled out Drew because all of his calls

and correspondence are carefully monitored," Jordan said a moment later. "And that's why I thought you might be doing this. I thought maybe you'd snapped or something."

Egan had come close to doing just that, but even if he had snapped, he wouldn't have gone after the people who'd gotten Shanna's organs. He would have gone after Drew.

And maybe Jordan.

But he hadn't snapped. And wouldn't. However, there were a couple of things that didn't fit here.

"If you thought I'd gone crazy, why were you heading out to the ranch?" Egan asked. "Weren't you afraid I'd gun you down once you got there?" Egan didn't bother to take the sarcasm out of his voice.

"I was going to see your brother, Court. I called dispatch, and they said you were still at work so I thought I could talk to Court alone."

Court was at the ranch all right, and his brother was not only a deputy sheriff, he would have also been more open to having a conversation with Jordan. Court probably didn't have the raw nerves that Egan still had about Shanna's death. Plus, Court and Jordan had been friends once, too.

"Look, I dismissed all of this at first," Jordan continued. "I'm a private investigator these days, and I know how to look at things objectively. Most things anyway," she added in a mumble.

Egan figured that was meant for him. Maybe Jordan hadn't been able to get past the hurt and emotions of Shanna's death, either, and that was why she'd thought Egan might be a killer.

"Have you been keeping an eye on Drew's brother, Kirk?" Egan asked.

Jordan nodded. Then, hesitated. "Well, as much as I can. He's a cattle broker, and he travels a lot. And yeah, he's still riled that his brother is on death row. He could be willing to play into Drew's sick fantasies of making sure every part of Shanna is dead."

Definitely a sick fantasy. And *riled* was putting it mildly for the way Kirk felt about his brother. Kirk thought Egan had provoked Drew into that hostage standoff. Kirk wasn't exactly specific about how Egan had managed to do that, but he blamed Egan for the situation. Maybe Kirk had decided to spread the blame around now and include Jordan. And those other recipients.

Still…

"What's the name and number of the SAPD officer who investigated the break-in and fire at your house?" he asked.

She paused several moments as if she might not tell him. That whole lack-of-trusting-him thing might be playing into this, but Jordan finally handed him her phone. "It's Christian Abrams. He's not the cop I contacted to come out here, but his number is in my recent calls."

It was. In fact, Jordan had called the man three times in the past two hours. And there were six missed calls from Christian to Jordan. It did make Egan wonder, though, why she hadn't phoned this guy after she had gotten injured. Or taken any of those six calls.

While Egan kept watch for the ambulance, he pressed Christian's number, and he answered right away. "Where the hell are you, Jordan?" the cop snarled.

"I'm not Jordan. I'm Egan McCall."

"The sheriff over in McCall Canyon," Christian said after a short pause, and Egan didn't think it was his imagination there was some venom in the man's tone. "Jordan went to you after all. I told her that wasn't a good idea."

Egan skipped right over that and went to

the reason he'd wanted to speak to the man. "Is someone trying to kill Jordan?"

Christian certainly didn't jump to answer that. "Is she there with you? Can she hear this?"

The answer to both of those was yes. Egan hadn't put the call on speaker, but the cop's voice was carrying in the truck. Jordan would almost certainly be able to hear him. But that wasn't what Egan said because he didn't want this guy clamming up.

"She can't hear us," Egan lied.

"Good. Because I don't want to alienate her. Jordan needs friends right now. The *right* friends."

Again, judging from the tone, Christian didn't think Egan fell into that category. "Did someone really break into her house and try to kill her?" Egan pressed.

"Yes, but Jordan has this notion—no, it's an obsession now—with connecting anything that's happening to her friend's murder. Did she tell you that she thinks someone is killing organ recipients?"

"She mentioned it."

"Well, I don't think it's true," Christian concluded. "I think Jordan's feeling so overwhelmed with guilt from her friend's death that she's seeing bogeymen who just aren't there."

Jordan's eyes narrowed, and she looked ready to snatch the phone from him, but Egan waved her off.

"You've investigated the two deaths?" Egan asked Christian.

"Yes, and I'm just not seeing what Jordan's seeing. One of the victims was mangled and burned so bad in a car accident that it was hard to tell if she had missing organs or not. The other was dumped in the woods, and animals had ravaged the body."

As gruesome as that was, Egan actually felt some relief. Maybe this wasn't connected to Shanna after all. Or maybe that was just wishful thinking on his part. It sickened him, though, to think that Jordan might be right, that Drew did indeed want any living part of Shanna dead.

"Look, just tell her to come home, and I'll talk this out with her," Christian continued. "Or better yet, tell me where she is, and I'll come and get her. I care for her. A lot. I want to make sure she gets the help she needs."

This time, Jordan did grab the phone,

and she hit the end-call button. She opened her mouth, no doubt to try to convince him that she wasn't "obsessed" as Christian had claimed. But the approaching headlights stopped her.

The vehicle wasn't coming from town but rather from the direction of the ranch. If it was Court or one of the hands, they would stop when they spotted his truck, and Egan would have to explain why Jordan was with him.

Too bad he wasn't sure of the answer himself.

As the headlights got closer, Egan felt his chest tighten. That was because it was a blue truck. Identical to his. And there wasn't another vehicle like it on the ranch. Plus, this vehicle had the same license plate number. Since Egan's plate was legit, this one had to be a fake.

"It's him." Jordan reached for his jeans. No doubt to try to get to her gun. But it was too late.

The bullet crashed through the windshield of Egan's truck.

Chapter Two

Jordan's breath froze. *No, please, no.* This couldn't be happening again.

She heard the hoarse sob tear from her throat, and she took hold of her gun that was in the back waistband of Egan's jeans. She managed to get it, but Egan immediately pushed her down onto the seat. Good thing, too.

Because the next bullet slammed into the seat right where Jordan had been sitting.

If Egan hadn't moved her at that exact moment, she'd be dead. She still might be, and this time the shooter might kill Egan right along with her.

"Hold on," Egan warned her. Keeping low, he started his truck, threw it into Reverse and jammed his foot on the accelerator.

The sudden jolt of motion knocked Jordan

against the seat. Hard. Her head hit, too, and the pain jolted through her. Still, feeling the awful pain was better than being shot again, but they weren't out of the woods yet.

A third bullet smacked into the windshield, and she could have sworn it missed Egan by less than an inch. The bullet went into the headrest next to where he was hunched down.

Jordan lifted her head to get a better look at the vehicle. It was the same truck, all right. And the person inside obviously wanted to have another go at killing her. The guy had the driver's-side window down, and he had a gun sticking out.

"I can't see his face," Jordan said. Because there was a dark tint on the windows. It didn't help, either, that the driver had on the high beams, and they were shining right in her eyes.

"Don't make it easy for him to shoot you," Egan snarled. He shoved her back down, and he kept speeding down the road in Reverse.

Jordan wanted to remind him that she was a PI and former cop. She could return fire. However, at the moment that might not even be true. She was dizzy from the pain, and her hands were shaking. It was possible she couldn't even hit the truck, much less the driver.

There was the sound of tires squealing against the asphalt, and Jordan knew what that meant. "He's coming after us."

Egan didn't confirm that, but since the shots had stopped, it told her that the driver might be the sole person in the truck. If so, it was a gutsy move on his part to go after two armed and trained people. Then again, the guy did have them on the run, and that driver had a lot more control over his vehicle right now than Egan did. It was easier to drive forward than in Reverse, but there was no place for them to turn around on the narrow road.

"Call nine-one-one," Egan ordered. "I want backup. But not the ambulance. Once we're out of this, I'll get you to the hospital."

Seeing a doctor was the least of her concerns right now, and Jordan made the call for backup. The problem wouldn't be getting someone out here because they weren't that far from town. But Egan was literally taking up most of the road, and it would make it hard for the deputies to get in position to help them. Still, she wasn't sure how much longer Egan could keep this up.

Jordan had just finished the call when she felt the jolt. The other truck had slammed into them. Hard. She heard the sound of metal scraping against metal. Unless the second truck had a reinforced bumper, he could be doing as much damage to his vehicle as he was to theirs.

Egan was still low in the seat, using the side mirror to navigate, but he had to adjust so he could better grip the steering wheel when the driver came at them again. If he hadn't done that, they would have gone into the ditch. It hadn't rained recently so it wasn't filled with water, but they'd still probably get stuck. Then, they'd be sitting ducks for the shooter.

The memories came. They always did whenever Jordan had a gun in her hand. That wasn't exactly an asset for a private investigator—to have the memories come at her so fast and strong that it put her on the verge of a panic attack. It was the reason she didn't wear a badge any longer. It was also the reason her life, and her head, were a mess.

If Drew Paxton was behind this, then he was getting a good laugh right now. Not only was he trying to "kill" any living piece of Shanna, he might manage to take out the man

Shanna had loved. Of course, Jordan felt as if she had already managed to "take out" Egan. Shanna's death had crushed him.

And Jordan was responsible for that.

Drew had been aiming at Jordan to finish her off when he'd fired that deadly shot. But he hadn't hit his target. Because Shanna had jumped in front of Jordan at the worst possible moment. And now Shanna was dead from a gunshot wound to the head, and Jordan was alive. Egan would never forgive her for that, and she'd never forgive herself.

The memories thankfully moved to the back of her mind when the truck crashed into them. Egan had to fight with the steering wheel again, and it didn't help when the driver rammed into them a fourth time. He would almost certainly continue to do that, too, until he disabled the engine, forcing them to stop. Then, he could try to use his gun on them to finish this.

"Hold on," Egan repeated to her.

Jordan lifted her head again so she could get a glimpse out the windshield, but the glass was so cracked and webbed that it was hard to see anything. She certainly couldn't tell if the guy was about to hit them again.

But she did hear the squeal of his tires.

Not the other truck's but Egan's. Egan hit the brakes, and in the same motion, he turned the steering wheel, backing onto what appeared to be a ranch trail. It was gravel, and the rocks pelted the undercarriage. The sound was deafening, like being bombarded with bullets, but it wasn't loud enough to drown out the other driver hitting his brakes, as well.

Now that they were both stopped, Jordan figured either Egan or she would have a shot. Of course, so would the driver of that truck. That was probably why Egan got his window down in a hurry. Before Jordan could even sit up, Egan got off two shots.

Jordan lowered her window, too, and she tried to steady her hand enough to take aim. She didn't get a chance to do that, though.

"What the hell," Egan mumbled.

The other truck's door flew open. Not on the driver's side, either. But the passenger's. Maybe she'd been wrong about the shooter being the only person inside the vehicle.

And then something fell from that opened door.

It was too dark to tell exactly what it was, but Jordan thought maybe it was a person. If it was someone, Jordan figured he or she would get up and start shooting at Egan and her.

But that didn't happen.

The driver of the other truck slammed on the accelerator, leaving the other person behind. Jordan braced herself for the truck to hit them again. It didn't. The driver sped off, heading in the direction of town.

She could practically feel the debate Egan was having with himself as to what to do. He volleyed his attention between the person on the ground and the escaping driver of the other truck.

Egan finally snatched his phone up from the seat, pressed a number and immediately put the call on speaker. No doubt so he could free up his hands in case he needed to use his gun.

"John," he said to the person who answered.

John Clary was one of the deputies who worked for Egan at the McCall Canyon Sheriff's Office. Jordan had known him for years, and she knew he was a good lawman. He had almost certainly brought another deputy with him, too.

"You've got a dark blue truck headed your way," Egan told the deputy. "It's identical to mine, right down to the same license plate, but it's not me. The driver is armed and dangerous. Stop him if you can."

"Will do. Say, are you okay, boss?" John asked.

Egan paused. "I have Jordan Gentry with me."

John obviously knew something had to be seriously wrong for her to be with Egan. And it was. That person on the road wasn't moving. That didn't mean he or she wasn't still dangerous, though. This could be a ploy to get Egan and her out in the open so the person could gun them down.

"Just get to the truck," Egan added to John a moment later. "I don't want whoever's inside escaping."

Neither did Jordan, but there were several ways the shooter could manage to do just that. She'd grown up in McCall Canyon and knew there were plenty of ranch trails between here and town. He could turn onto one of those and hide. Plus, there was even another farm road along the route. If he or she managed to get there ahead of the deputy, then it was just a short drive to the interstate. It would be hard to track him after that because she was betting he would switch out those fake plates.

Part of her didn't mind having some distance between the attacker and her. Especially since Jordan wasn't in much shape to put up a fight. Her shoulder was still bleeding, and her head was throbbing. But she also knew if they didn't catch him now, that he would likely come after her again.

"No matter what happens, I want you to stay put," Egan warned her a split second before he eased the truck out from the trail and back onto the road. "And keep an eye out in case our *friend* returns to shoot at us again."

Jordan was already doing that, but she was also making glances at the person who was still lying on the road. Egan pulled closer, but it was still hard to tell much because he or she was wrapped in a blanket. Of course, the cover could be concealing a weapon.

Had Drew or his brother managed to send would-be killers after them? If so, this could be a hired gun. That was probably why Egan hadn't wanted her out of the truck. But obviously he wasn't going to take that same precaution himself.

He put on his emergency flashers, the red lights knifing through the darkness, and he pulled to a stop directly next to the person.

Jordan moved closer to him so she could provide some backup if this turned into a shootout, but there wasn't much she could do to keep him out of the line of fire.

Egan stepped out.

He immediately maneuvered himself so that he was in front of Jordan, protecting her. She knew it wasn't personal, though. Egan was a lawman through and through, and he would now see her as part of the job.

Even if it wasn't a job that he especially wanted.

Jordan moved again, too, so that she could keep watch around them and still see from over his shoulder. With his gun ready, Egan walked closer. There was still no movement, so he used the toe of his boot to nudge the person.

"Is it a dummy?" Jordan asked.

Egan nudged it again and shook his head. "There's blood."

Sweet heaven. That gave Jordan another jolt of adrenaline—along with a really bad thought. Both Egan and she had fired shots into the truck. And they'd done that before the person had been dumped on the road.

Had she shot him or her?

Or had Egan done it?

Jordan forced herself to remember that this could have been the shooter who'd been trying to kill them. He or she might have deserved to die. But like Shanna, the person could have been innocent in all of this, too.

Her lungs started to ache, and that was when she realized she was holding her breath. Her chest muscles were too tight. As if they were squeezing the life out of her. Jordan refused to give in to the memories and the panic. None of that would help Egan right now.

She heard Egan gut out some profanity under his breath as he reached for the blanket. He didn't yank it but rather gave it a gentle tug, touching it only with his fingertips.

The way a cop would touch evidence he didn't want contaminated.

And Jordan soon realized why Egan had done that. The moment he pulled back the blanket, she saw the face of the person who was wrapped inside it.

It was a woman.

And she was dead.

Chapter Three

Egan couldn't push away the sickening feeling of dread. A woman was dead. And he might have been the one to kill her.

"There was no ID on the body," Egan heard Court say from the other end of the line. "We'll try to match her prints so we can figure out who she is."

His brother was at the crime scene with the medical examiner and the CSI team so Court would make sure that everything was done as fast as it could be. Egan had wanted to be there, too, but he also had to make sure Jordan got to the hospital.

And that she was safe.

Ironic, since just an hour ago he hadn't believed she was truly in danger. Well, he sure as heck believed it now. The person in the truck had wanted to kill her. He was certain about that. But the next steps were for Egan to figure out who this dead Jane Doe was and how she fit into what had happened.

Obviously, Jordan wanted to hear all about that, as well. Even though the doctor was stitching up her shoulder, she was leaning closer to Egan. No doubt trying to hear Court's every word. When he finished the call, Egan would give her the condensed version, but first he wanted to try to process it himself.

"Cause of death?" Egan asked Court.

"Two gunshot wounds to the head. No stippling."

Hell.

Stippling happened when particles of gunpowder embedded into the skin. Since it wasn't on the victim, Egan knew she probably hadn't been shot at point-blank range. That meant, she might have still been alive while she was in the truck. *Might.*

Egan dreaded this next question, but he had to know. "Did the victim have any organs missing?"

Court blurted out a single word of bad profanity. "No. Not that I can see. Why would you think that?"

"I'll fill you in when you're back here."

No way did Egan want to get into this over the phone, but it was a relief that the woman seemed to be intact. "Were there exit wounds on the body?" Egan asked.

"No. The bullets are still in her."

As grisly as that sounded, that was actually a good thing. "I want ballistics done ASAP," Egan reminded his brother.

Though a reminder really wasn't necessary. Court was already well aware that was one answer they had to have right away.

"I'll get it," Court assured him. "You do know, though, that even if the shot came from your gun, or Jordan's, this was an accident? From everything you told me, both of you were aiming at the driver, who was shooting at you. You didn't even know there was a passenger in the vehicle."

Yeah, he knew that in his head. But his gut was having a lot of trouble with it. If the woman had died from his bullet, then the bottom line was that he'd been the one to kill her.

"Also, I've made some calls about the truck the gunman was driving," Egan continued a moment later. "It had to be custom since the windshield was bullet resistant and the front end had been reinforced. We might get lucky and find out who ordered a vehicle like that."

"I can help you with that when I get back to the office," Court answered. "Might not be for a while, though, since we want to process Jordan's vehicle, too. How is she, by the way?" Court asked after a pause.

She had a lot less blood on her than when Egan had first seen her, but she had that stark look in her eyes. The one that told him she was dealing with a serious adrenaline crash and was maybe in shock.

"Jordan's, well, Jordan," Egan settled for saying. Stubborn and driven. Not necessarily a good combination.

"She really should be in the hospital," Dr. Lucy Madison said to Egan the moment he was finished with his call.

Dr. Madison had been working at McCall Canyon Hospital since Egan was a boy. She knew her stuff. And she was right. Jordan should be in the hospital, but when she'd repeatedly refused, Egan had brought her to the sheriff's office instead and called Dr. Madison to come and check her out.

"I'd rather not be at the hospital with a killer on the loose," Jordan grumbled.

It wasn't her first grumble about that, either, and Egan could definitely see her side of it. Jordan was a former cop and hadn't been able to stop the attack, and this thug could just come walking into the hospital to finish what he'd started. At least Egan could control who came in and out of the sheriff's office, and the gunman would have to be plenty stupid to come into a building with cops.

"Will she be okay?" Egan asked Dr. Madison. It wasn't a general kind of question, though. He needed to know how soon he could move her to a safe location so he could get on with this investigation.

"I think she'll be all right," the doc answered. "I'd still like to run some tests, but if it's absolutely necessary for her to be here, it can wait."

"It's necessary," Jordan assured her.

Dr. Madison made a suit-yourself sound and gathered up her things. "I'll call in a script for some pain meds, but something tells me you won't be taking them."

Jordan looked at her. "I won't be." And there wasn't a shred of doubt in her voice.

The doctor sighed. "Well, just take some

over-the-counter stuff if it gets too bad. You'll have a doozy of a headache for a day or two."

Egan figured from the way Jordan kept wincing that it'd gone well past the *doozy* stage. Still, he didn't press it. But he would when the doctor was finally out of his office.

"I will need my immunosuppressant meds, though," Jordan told the doctor. "They're at my place in San Antonio, but I haven't had my dose today."

"Immunosuppressant?" Egan asked.

Jordan dodged his gaze. "For the kidney transplant." She gave the name of the drugs to the doctor.

Dr. Madison nodded. "I'll get you a new script. Will she be here for the next hour or so?" she asked Egan. "Because if so, I can have the pharmacy deliver it to her. Jordan really shouldn't miss taking it even for a day. It could cause her body to reject the donor kidney."

Egan wasn't sure he'd wanted to know that. It was always hard to think of Jordan having part of Shanna inside her. If that part died, it'd be a little like losing Shanna all over again. That probably didn't make sense to most people, which was why Egan kept it to himself.

"Jordan will be here for a while," Egan assured the doctor. Just how long "a while" was, though, he wouldn't know until he'd learned more about what was going on.

"Tell me about the other two living recipients," Egan said to Jordan once the doctor had left.

Jordan had already given him the names—Tori Judd and Irene Adair—and while Egan had been making some calls, he'd done internet searches on them, but he hadn't pulled up much. Irene Adair didn't even have a driver's license so there was no DMV photo on her. He had gotten a look at a photo of Tori, but Egan didn't know if she was a match to the dead woman or not.

Jordan drew in a deep breath and moved from the corner of his desk where she'd been sitting to the chair across from him. "I have computer files on both of them, but I honestly don't know if one of them is the dead woman. There was too much blood for me to get a good look at her face."

Ditto. But what he had been able to see would be etched in his mind forever. So would some of the details that were eating away at him. "I'm not sure our attacker had enough time to wrap her in a blanket before he dumped her out of the truck."

"Yes." Jordan said it so quickly that she'd probably given it some thought. But then she lifted her shoulder. "Unless she'd already had the blanket draped around her." She winced again. Hesitated. "Did the woman have a missing heart or pancreas?"

"No."

Egan saw the same relief in her eyes that he'd felt when Court had told him that. Like him, the relief didn't last long.

"It's possible the gunman had the woman on the seat next to him," Jordan said, "and he pushed her out only after she'd been shot."

Egan had considered that, too. That was why they needed to find the driver of that truck so he could shed some light on this.

"How long before we have ballistics?" she asked.

Egan nearly told her there was no "we" in this investigation, but there was. Whether he liked it or not, and he didn't, Jordan and he were in this together.

"As soon as the ME can get the bullet out of the Jane Doe, Court can do the comparison with our guns."

Egan had gone ahead and sent both his and Jordan's weapons to the lab. Still, it might be tomorrow before they heard anything. It might be that long as well before they got an ID on the woman. It'd be hell waiting, but it wouldn't be downtime.

"I've already called Kirk," Egan continued. "He didn't answer, but I left a message for him to get in here for questioning."

"He won't like that," she said under her breath.

No. But then Kirk didn't care much for anything Egan did. Kirk apparently wasn't objective enough to figure out the only person to blame for Shanna's murder was Drew himself.

"Kirk is obviously a suspect," Egan went on, "but I have to wonder why he'd wait nearly two years before doing something like this."

Jordan gave a frustrated sigh. "Maybe it's just now sinking in that his brother is going to die on death row. Or Drew could consider this a loose end he wants tied up before he gets that lethal injection. He lost his appeal."

True. But there'd be other appeals. Ones that would take a long time. The average inmate in Texas spent over ten years on death row. It didn't matter that there'd been eyewitnesses to what Drew had done. It didn't matter that the man wrecked plenty of lives. He would still survive years longer than Shanna. Justice definitely wasn't a substitute for the havoc that had played out that day.

"I also need to know if there's someone else you've crossed paths with," Egan went on. "Someone you ticked off enough to do something like this. Because what happened tonight might not even be related to the two dead recipients."

Jordan didn't argue with that verbally, but she did shake her head. "I'm not seeing anyone."

He waited for her to add more. When she didn't, Egan went with his next question. "How about the cop, Christian Abrams? He said he cared about you *a lot.*"

Her mouth tightened. "He thinks I'm crazy. I'm not."

Egan was beginning to believe that. "Could something have happened between you two to make him want you dead?"

"No." But then she huffed. "We worked together when I was still on the force. Now I do death penalty case reviews for a watchdog group called The Right Verdict. They want to make sure people haven't been wrongly convicted, and Christian is still my main contact at SAPD. He and I have had a disagreement or two about whether or not someone incarcerated actually got a fair shake at justice. But other than that, nothing."

That didn't seem like much of a red flag to turn a cop into a killer. Still, it was worth checking out. Egan pushed a notepad and pen across the desk toward her. "Give me the names of the cases where you disagreed."

The surprise flashed through her eyes. "You don't really believe Christian could have done this?"

"I won't know until I've checked him out." He tipped his head to the notepad. "Names, dates, anything else you have."

Jordan hesitated a moment and then wrote down a website address and password. "That will get you into my online storage account. The first file will be everything about the organ recipients. The next two will be the case files I'm working on for my job, the ones where Christian and I didn't see eye to eye."

Good. He put the note with the info in his pocket so he could go through that while he was setting up a safe house for Jordan. He was about to broach that subject with her, but Jordan spoke before he could say anything.

"One of the calls you made while I was being stitched up was to Alma Lawton. She's the woman who'd had an affair with your father, Warren."

Obviously, Jordan had been keeping tabs on him. Of course, that wouldn't have been hard to do since his father's affair had made the newspapers. It had come to light after Warren had been shot and nearly killed. His father had led a double life for over thirty years, and his lover, Alma, had been a suspect. Initially so had her and Warren's son, Raleigh. Egan's half brother. But both had since been cleared.

"Alma has an alibi for tonight," Egan explained. "And the rangers are monitoring her bank accounts. If she'd withdrawn any money for a hired gun, we would have known about it."

"But if you called her, you must have thought she could possibly be involved in this," Jordan pointed out.

Egan shrugged. "Just ruling her out. That's why I'll check into Christian, the living recipients and the cases you're reviewing for your job."

She looked up and their eyes connected. For just a moment he saw the fear and pain—something she quickly tried to rein in. He saw something else, too. Jordan, the woman. She was attractive. Always had been. And she'd always had a thing for him since way back in high school.

That "thing" she had for him was apparently still there.

Egan figured that was because Jordan and he had been each other's first lovers. That sort of thing created weird bonds between people. But the bond hadn't kept Jordan in McCall Canyon. She'd always wanted to be a big-city cop and had left Egan behind. It had hurt at the time, but they'd both moved on. And Egan had eventually met Shanna and fallen in love with her.

During the time he'd been with Shanna, Egan hadn't felt the old attraction for Jordan. But he darn sure felt it now. Felt it and shoved it aside as fast as he could. It wasn't hard to do because of the voice he heard in the squad room. Apparently, it was a voice Jordan recognized, too, because she pulled back her shoulders and slowly got to her feet.

Their visitor was Leeroy Sullivan, Shanna's father.

As Egan usually did when it came to Leeroy, he gathered his breath and got ready for battle. Leeroy would never just pay him a casual visit, and since it was well past normal duty hours, something must be wrong. Of course, often the only thing that was wrong was that Leeroy was drunk and wanted to vent. However, Egan didn't see any signs of drunkenness tonight.

Simply put, Leeroy had not aged well. He was in his early fifties, but looked ten years older than that. And he'd let himself go, too. Once he'd been a big college football star and careful about keeping in shape. All of that had gone by the wayside, though, when he'd lost his only child. Shanna had been the center of his life.

"Egan," Leeroy greeted. It wasn't friendly. Never was when it came to Leeroy. He blamed Egan for Shanna's dying. But judging from the glare he shot Jordan, she had top dibs in the blame department.

"I heard you were here," Leeroy said to her. He spared a glance at the bruise on her head.

"How'd you hear that?" Egan asked.

"My wife was in the ER with a stomach bug, and I heard the nurses talking about Doc Madison having to come over here and stitch up Jordan. The gossip is that someone attacked her." Leeroy didn't sound choked up about that.

"Someone did," Jordan said, but she had to clear her throat and repeat it to give it some sound. Obviously, she didn't like dealing with Shanna's father any more than Egan did. "The person shot at Egan, too."

Definitely not choked up about that, either. Leeroy's scowl stayed in place.

Since Egan wasn't in the mood for getting into a scowling match with Leeroy, Egan just laid it all out there. "If you were hoping Jordan and I would be killed, you didn't get your wish."

Leeroy didn't jump to deny that was indeed his wish. And it might be.

"I came to tell Jordan that I don't want any more visits from her cop friend," Leeroy finally said. "In fact, I don't want anything to do with her or anyone else who considers her a friend."

Leeroy let his scowl linger a bit on Egan, probably because he likely thought that friendship label applied to him simply because he was standing next to Jordan.

Jordan shook her head. "What cop visited you?" she asked Leeroy.

"Christian Abrams."

Egan looked at her to see if she'd known about that, but she obviously hadn't. He definitely didn't like the way the cop's name had come up twice now.

"What did Christian want?" she pressed.

"To tell me some cockamamie story about the folks that got Shanna's organs, that somebody was killing them off. He didn't believe it. Neither do I. But he said he was worried about you going off the deep end over it. I told him I didn't give a rat whether you went crazy or not."

Later Egan would find out why Christian would make a visit like that to Shanna's father, but for now, he wanted to address the pure venom he'd just heard in Leeroy's voice.

"You hate Jordan that much," Egan commented.

"I hate you just as much." Leeroy's face was tight with anger, but he seemed to be blinking back tears, too. "If it hadn't been for you two, my baby would be alive. You two let her get killed." His attention slashed back to Jordan. "Shanna took a shot that was meant for you. That bullet should have gone into you."

"A bullet did go into Jordan," Egan reminded the man. Even though it did feel strange defending Jordan. Still, she wasn't defending herself. "It damaged both of her kidneys, remember?"

"I remember," Leeroy spat out. "But Jordan got the easy bullet. My baby took the one that should have killed Jordan instead. And she died. My baby died. Jordan lived because she got a part of Shanna. So did those other people, and it's not right."

Egan latched right on to that. "Are you saying the recipients should have died, too?"

He didn't say it with actual words, but his expression confirmed it. Leeroy's feelings weren't much of a surprise to Egan. That didn't mean hearing it didn't sting, though. It did. Because Leeroy was right. Still, that much hurt and anger was a red flag to a lawman.

"I gotta ask," Egan said to him. "Where were you tonight?"

The jolt of surprise seemed to make Leeroy's muscles even tighter. "Oh, no. You're not going to try to pin this on me."

"It was a simple question," Egan pointed out. "Usually it's simple to answer for someone who isn't hiding anything."

If looks could have killed, Leeroy would have ended Egan's life right there. "Like I said, I was at the ER with my wife. If you don't believe me, just ask the nurses."

Oh, he would. But Egan wouldn't like doing it. Plain and simple, he felt guilty when it came to Leeroy. He hadn't protected Shanna, and part of Egan would always believe that he deserved every bit of hatred and venom that Leeroy sent his way.

"Tell that cop friend to stay away from me," Leeroy growled to Jordan before he turned and stormed out.

"I'll call Christian," she said, taking out her phone.

She wasn't scowling exactly, but Egan knew from her tone that this wouldn't be a pleasant conversation. However, it was one he wanted to hear. He didn't get to do that because his own phone rang, and Egan knew he had to take the call when he saw Court's name on the screen.

"No ID yet on the Jane Doe," Court volunteered the moment Egan answered. "But when the ME and his crew were moving the body, something fell out of the blanket. I bagged it, but I thought you might want to see it before I send it to the crime lab."

"Why? What is it?"

Egan thought he heard his brother mumble some curse words. "It's a note," Court finally said. "It's not good, Egan. And it's addressed to Jordan and you."

Chapter Four

Jordan had no trouble hearing what Court had just said to Egan, and it caused everything inside her to go still. For a couple of seconds anyway. Then the new wave of panic came. And pain. But the pain was because she'd bunched up her forehead, the motion pulling at the stitches.

It was a reminder she didn't need of just how close she'd come to dying tonight. The note was perhaps going to be another of those unnecessary prompts.

Since the note was addressed to Egan and her, that meant the attack and the woman's death weren't just some fluke, that they did indeed have something to do with them. Of course, she hadn't actually believed that it was a sick coincidence, but she'd held on to the hope like a lifeline.

Well, that lifeline was gone now.

And Jordan just sat there, trying to gather what little of her composure she had left so she could listen to the rest of what Court had to say. Judging from Egan's grimace and his muttered profanity, he was trying to do the same thing.

"The note's handwritten," Court went on. "It's scrawled as if the person wrote it in a hurry. It says, 'Want to put an end to the killings? Meet me. I'll be calling you soon.' And there's no signature."

That last part definitely wasn't a surprise. No way would the person who'd written that note want them to know who he or she was. Because if they did know, Egan could make an arrest for attempted murder. Maybe even murder. But the jury was still out on who'd killed that woman who'd been dumped from the truck.

"I'll be calling you soon," Court repeated. "You think this could be a situation where this clown is going to demand payment so the killings will stop?"

"Maybe." Though Egan didn't sound especially hopeful about that.

Neither was Jordan, but it was sadly the

best-case scenario here. If the person could be paid off, then the motive was simply money. Not that she had money, but Egan did, and plenty of people knew that. Still, this didn't feel like something that simple. It would be a lot harder for them to stop this guy if the motive was revenge because their attacker might not be satisfied until Egan and she were dead.

She stood and started walking, just to give herself something to do with the slam of fresh adrenaline she got. Egan's office wasn't that big so she soon ended up in front of the bookcase and filing cabinet, where there were framed pictures of his family.

And Shanna, of course.

Every detail of Shanna's features was etched in Jordan's memory, but it was even more painful seeing that face. That smile. Jordan went back to the chair so the photos would be out of sight and hopefully out of mind. For a couple of seconds anyway. She needed to regain her footing, and she didn't stand a chance of doing that if she was looking at Shanna's face.

"Are you okay?" Court pressed when neither of them said anything.

"Fine," Egan snapped, but all three of them

knew that wasn't the truth. "Have the hand-writing on the note analyzed. Also check the paper for prints or trace."

"I will," Court assured him. "But I think this makes it pretty clear that Jordan and you are the targets. Please tell me you won't go to a meeting with this snake if he or she actually calls."

A muscle flickered in Egan's jaw. "If there is a call, I'll see what he wants and take things from there."

Judging from Court's huff, he didn't like that answer, but Jordan felt the same way as Egan. If a meeting truly would put a stop to the killings, then she would go for it. Well, if she could figure out a way for Egan and her to come out of it alive.

"It's late, and I'm sure you're both ex-hausted. Are you taking Jordan to the ranch?" Court asked a moment later.

There was more of that muscle flickering from Egan. "Maybe. But if that's where we go, it would be just for tonight."

Jordan was shaking her head before he even finished, and she got to her feet. "I don't want to go there," she protested.

Egan didn't even acknowledge that. He just

kept talking to his brother. "Call me the minute you get anything back from the ME, CSIs or the lab. Are there any safety measures you want me to take for Rayna?"

"Rayna and I have already worked that out." And Court proceeded to tell Egan about some hands standing guard and an armed security system.

Jordan knew that Rayna was a local horse trainer who was also engaged to Court. That likely meant the woman had already moved to the ranch, and Jordan figured she could use that to win the argument she was about to have with Egan. An argument that started the moment he finished the call with Court.

"I don't want to go to the McCall Ranch," she repeated. "Your family will be there. Your father, your sister and apparently Rayna, too. My being there could put them in danger. Not to mention that none of them will want me there after what happened to Shanna."

"No, my family won't be there. Court and Rayna have their own place on the back of the property. My sister, Rachel, lives with her soon-to-be husband in a house near town. And my dad has been staying at his fishing cabin down by the river."

Even though she wasn't ready to give up her argument, that did give her a new reason for alarm. That was because the fishing cabin was a good mile from the main ranch house.

"Is it safe for your father to be there?" she asked. "I mean since someone tried to kill him just two months ago."

Egan lifted his shoulder. "Some people ignore the danger and hope that it doesn't come back to bite them."

"You mean me."

"Yeah," he readily admitted. "Just because you didn't die with Shanna doesn't mean you have to choose to die now."

Surprised, Jordan pulled back her shoulders. Egan didn't usually bring up Shanna's name around her. Nor did he usually show any kind of concern for her. Of course, maybe the concern was because of the danger she might have brought to his doorstep.

"You blame me for what happened tonight?" she came out and asked.

"No," he snapped, but it certainly sounded as if he meant yes. "It was beyond risky, though, for you to investigate those other deaths on your own. You should have turned all of this over to the cops before things got this far."

She heard the words and was certain that they were true, but there was another angle to this. "You didn't believe me when I told you about the other deaths. You thought I'd gone off the deep end."

And maybe he still did think that, but Egan managed to give her a flat stare. "You really want whoever's behind this to get his hands on you?"

"No. Of course not." It put an icy chill through her just thinking about it. This person had likely killed three people, and she didn't want her or anyone else to be his next victim. "The same goes for you, though. We need a safe house, not your family's ranch."

"That's probably true, but it's nearly midnight and too late to come up with an alternative."

She tipped her head toward the back of the building. "How about the break room? There used to be a shower and a sofa back there."

The last time she'd seen it, it had definitely qualified as bare-bones. Nothing more than a flop room for cops pulling double shifts. Still, it beat going back outside. She didn't want to run from a killer, but Jordan wasn't sure she could face him head-on right now.

Egan stared at her, and she saw the fatigue and weariness in not only his eyes but in every part of his body. He probably needed to crash for at least a nap anyway. Still, she doubted either of them would get much sleep no matter where they were.

He took out his phone again, and he fired off a text. "I'll have one of the hands bring us a change of clothes and some toiletries. Some dinner, too." He motioned for her to follow him.

And that was when Jordan realized she had actually won the argument with Egan. Too bad it didn't exactly feel like a win. Every part of her was on edge, and apparently it was the same for Egan because when the front door opened, he reached for his gun. So did Ian Meade, the deputy who was at his desk in the squad room. But their visitor wasn't the killer. Or if it was, he was wearing a white lab coat.

Jordan didn't recognize him, but Egan and Ian must have because they both huffed and reholstered their weapons.

"It's okay," Egan said to her, and he blew

out a quick breath. "That's Billy Watson. He works at the pharmacy."

Billy nodded and volleyed uneasy glances at all three of them. "Uh, Dr. Madison asked me to bring over these meds." Billy handed Egan the small white bag, and he in turn gave it to Jordan.

Jordan thanked him, but Billy didn't hang around. He got out of there, fast, probably because he'd figured there must be some potential trouble for Egan and Ian to have drawn so fast.

Egan took a laptop from one of the desks and got her moving again toward the break room, but this time it was Ian who stopped them. He gave Egan a thick file. "You said you wanted to go through that," Ian commented. "I can do it for you. I mean, you need to get some rest."

Jordan didn't know what was in that file, but Egan didn't take Ian up on his offer. He simply told the deputy to come and get him if there was any hint of a problem, and he led Jordan to the break room.

Yes, it was as bare-bones as she had remembered with a kitchenette, sofa and chair. The attached bathroom wasn't much bigger than a storage closet. Egan put the file and laptop on a small table next to the chair.

"You can take the couch," she said when he took several blankets and pillows from one of the lockers.

"I'm not the one who got shot tonight." He motioned to the bag that the medic had brought and dropped the bedding on the sofa. "Take your meds and get some rest." Egan immediately poured himself a cup of coffee, took it to the chair and opened the file.

"If you're drinking coffee, you must not be planning on getting any sleep," she pointed out.

He made a sound of agreement and started thumbing through the papers in the file. Since he obviously wasn't in a chatting mood, Jordan grabbed a bottle of water so she could take the pills, but instead of heading straight to the sofa, she walked in Egan's direction to get a look at what had captured his attention.

And her stomach went to her knees.

Because the first thing she saw was a picture of a dead woman. Even though it was impossible to tell the woman's identity from the photo alone, the name was beneath the grisly image.

Breanna Culver.

The woman who'd gotten Shanna's liver. Receiving that organ had saved Breanna's life, but she certainly wasn't alive in the photo. The shot had been taken after the horrific car wreck that had killed her.

Egan looked up at her, and while he didn't look especially pleased about her looming over him, he didn't close the file or tell her to move away.

"When the doctor was examining you, I texted Ian to print out everything on the other two dead women," Egan explained.

Yes, but there seemed to be more in that file than just that. When he moved aside another page, she saw the police report on Shanna's murder.

Jordan had read it, of course. Actually, she could probably tell him word for word everything that was in it. But she couldn't figure out why Egan was looking at it now. Certainly, he didn't want all those painful memories brought to the surface at a time like this. Maybe, though, the memories were always with him.

They were always with her.

"I have to look at all the angles," he said.

"What happened tonight and what happened to those other two women might be linked to Shanna. Or someone could just want it to appear as if it is."

She thought about that a moment. "You're talking about Christian now."

He didn't need to confirm that, but since they were on the subject of the possibly dirty cop, she opened up the laptop and made her way to the online files.

"I don't like that Christian went to visit Leeroy," Egan added a moment later.

Neither did Jordan, and she'd considered calling Christian about that. But it could wait. The numbing medication was wearing off from where she'd had her stitches, and the wound was starting to throb. Best if she had a clear head when she confronted Christian. And it would indeed be a confrontation since he had no right to go to Leeroy with any of this.

She opened the computer files where she'd had some crossover with Christian and passed the laptop to Egan. "Like I said, I do death penalty reviews. Just to make sure corners weren't cut, etc. And those are the two cases I flagged. Both were arrests that Christian made."

Egan immediately began to read through them. "What made you suspicious about them?"

Jordan hoped this didn't make her sound foolish. "Gut feeling. Christian was the only officer on scene for both arrests. Both of the prisoners claimed he set them up. I know, a lot of people in prison insist that happened," she added. "But this just felt like something I should look at a little closer."

Egan lifted his head and made eye contact with her. "And Christian knows about these *closer looks*?"

She nodded. "I think he'd like for me to back off, but that, of course, only makes me want to dig deeper."

Egan made another of those sounds of agreement and went back to reading the file. The reading, though, came to an abrupt halt, and she saw him go stiff. "Christian was supposed to be one of the officers on scene the night Shanna was murdered."

Yes, that was in her notes. "He said something personal came up, and he asked another officer to fill in for him." She paused. "Christian knew Shanna, of course, because she was a parole officer in San Antonio, but I think that's the only connection between them."

If there was something else, Jordan hadn't been able to find it. And she'd looked—hard.

Egan continued to stare up at her, and she saw the concerns and questions in his eyes. At least that was what was there. But it changed a little when his attention dropped to her mouth. He frowned as if disgusted with himself.

"Go ahead and get some sleep," he insisted. He set the file that Ian had given him aside. "I'll get to work on finding a safe house for you. The marshals can take over protective custody until we figure out what's going on."

He was putting some distance between them. That was a good thing, Jordan reminded herself, even if it suddenly made her feel worse than she already did. It made her ache for the closeness that Egan and she had once had.

She moved away from him, going to the sofa. No way would she get any sleep tonight, but it was obvious that Egan wanted the space between them to happen right now. However, Jordan had barely managed to get settled on the makeshift bed when the sound of Egan's phone ringing cut through the room. Since it could be an update on the case, she immediately sat back up.

"It's Court," Egan relayed to her when he looked at the screen. He dragged in a deep breath. The kind of breath people took when they were bracing themselves for bad news. He answered the call and put it on speaker.

"Still no sign of the shooter," Court said the moment he was on the line. "But we did find out more about the body." Court hesitated. "The ME took pictures, but I'm not sure this is something you should see. Jordan, either."

That got her attention, and she came off the sofa so she could go back across the room to Egan.

Egan ground out some profanity. "I've seen pictures of dead bodies before." His voice was edged with sarcasm.

"Not this dead body," Court practically whispered.

"Just send it," Egan insisted. "And tell me what the heck this is all about."

Court certainly didn't jump into an explanation. "There was…damage to the body. Damage not caused by the bullet." He hesitated again. Then groaned. "I think we're dealing with a very sick serial killer."

Chapter Five

Egan kept his eyes closed and pretended to be asleep when he heard Jordan get up from the sofa and go into the bathroom. A moment later, he heard her turn on the shower. He'd already taken one about an hour earlier, but it hadn't helped soothe his knotted muscles as he'd hoped it would.

Of course, nothing was going to soothe him right now.

Over the past six hours or so, he'd managed a few catnaps while sprawled out in the chair, but it hadn't been anywhere near a peaceful sleep. He'd had the nightmares again. Those images of Shanna being shot, and dying. But now he had a new image to add to the hellish mix.

The photo from the medical examiner that Court had sent him.

His brother had warned him that it was something he shouldn't see, but Egan hadn't exactly had a choice about that. He was the sheriff, and he needed every detail of this investigation. And now he had to figure out how to get that specific detail out of his head.

Not only the dead woman. But also the damage that'd been done to her heart.

Court had said they were dealing with a sick serial killer, and after seeing that picture, Egan had to agree with him. Well, unless someone was trying to trick them into believing they were dealing with a madman. If that was indeed what was happening, it was going to take some concrete evidence to start unraveling all of this.

They still didn't have a positive ID on the dead woman yet, but Egan thought she might be Tori Judd, the woman who received Shanna's heart. Her heart had still been there in the woman's body, but she'd been stabbed multiple times. The stab wounds were injuries that the medical examiner had thought might be postmortem. So, if the person responsible wanted them to believe they were dealing with someone vindictive, then he or she was doing a stellar job.

The silver lining in all of this was the other living recipient, Irene Adair, was alive and well. Court had finally managed to track her down while the woman was finishing up a vacation with her boyfriend.

When he heard Jordan turn off the shower, Egan went ahead and got up to start a fresh pot of coffee. He already felt wired, but he stood no chance of making it through the day until he tanked up on more caffeine.

He poured himself a cup as soon as it was ready, but he was still on his first sip when his phone dinged with another call. Something that had been happening most of the night. This time it was Thea Morris, his day-shift deputy.

"Some good news," Thea greeted. "Just got back the report from the lab, and our Jane Doe was killed with a .38-caliber bullet."

Yeah, that was good news, and Egan released the breath he'd been holding. Since both Jordan and he had used .40-caliber ammo, it meant they hadn't killed the woman with friendly fire. That didn't help the woman, of course, but Egan had enough worry and guilt hanging over him without adding this to the mix. He was certain that Jordan did, too.

And speaking of Jordan, she came out of the bathroom, and she was wearing the loaner jeans and blue top that one of the ranch hands had brought over for her. The clothes no doubt belonged to his sister because they weren't a good fit for Jordan. They were snug, practically clinging to her body.

Something that Egan wished he hadn't noticed.

While he was wishing, he would have preferred not to feel the kick from the old attraction. Talk about bad timing. Even if he'd wanted to renew a relationship with Jordan—and he didn't—he definitely didn't need to be reminded of why they'd once been lovers.

She kept her attention on him when she poured herself some coffee, and so that she wouldn't feel the need to come closer to hear his phone conversation, Egan put the call on speaker.

But Jordan came closer anyway. "Is that Thea?" she mouthed.

Since the bathroom was only a few feet away from where they were standing, it was possible Jordan had already heard his side of the conversation. Just in case she hadn't, Egan filled her in. He filled in Thea, too.

"Jordan's back in the room with me," he told Thea, just so the deputy would know that someone else was listening to their conversation. "The shots that killed the woman didn't come from our guns," he added to Jordan.

He saw the relief go through her eyes and the rest of her. Jordan didn't exactly relax, but her shoulders loosened up a little. "Has there been any progress on confirming the identity of the dead woman?" Jordan asked.

"No. Still no ID," Thea answered. "Court said we were going with the theory that this was Tori Judd, but we're having trouble getting her dental records. Her dentist didn't respond to our calls, but his office should open in a couple of hours."

True. It was nearly seven now, but even after they made the request for the records, it still might take a while for a match to be determined. "How about the check on Tori? Did that turn up anything?"

"Nothing. San Antonio PD sent officers to her house just as you requested, but she wasn't there. She lives alone, and her parents don't know where she is, either."

Probably because the woman was dead. If and when they had that confirmed, then it would be time to start interviewing anyone who might have something to do with this. That meant starting with Kirk and Leeroy. Christian, too, since Egan had plenty of questions about the cop's possible involvement in this.

Whatever *this* was.

It was hard to swallow that someone might be trying to make sure no part of Shanna lived on. But that might be exactly what was happening here. If so, then Kirk and/or Leeroy had to be at the top of his suspect list. Kirk because this might be a way of getting revenge for his murdering brother, and Leeroy because he was well past the grieving-father stage.

"Kirk Paxton should be coming in for questioning in about an hour," Thea went on. "I doubt you got much sleep last night so you want one of the other deputies or me to do the interview?"

It was tempting to hand that off, but Egan really wanted to see Kirk's face when he asked him about the dead woman. And asked him if he had an alibi. "No. I'll do it. How about the search of Kirk's place?"

That was something else that Egan had

also requested in the wee hours of the morning. Not just for Kirk but for Leeroy, too. He wanted their houses checked for any signs of that custom truck or the murder weapon.

"The searches should be starting soon," Thea answered. "We're using reserve deputies for that." She paused, and he heard the clicks of her computer keyboard. "I got the visitors' log from the warden at the prison where Drew's incarcerated a couple of minutes before I called you, but nothing stands out. In the past month, he saw Kirk once and his lawyer twice. He didn't answer any of his fan mail. Yeah, he gets fan mail," Thea said in a grumble.

Egan knew about that, too, but anytime it came up, it ate away at him. Drew had murdered an innocent woman and nearly killed a second one, and there were sick idiots out there who worshipped him for that. He'd gotten more than a dozen marriage proposals.

"I asked the warden to go back another two months for the visitors' records," Thea continued. "I know you've been keeping up with it, but it might be worth another look."

It was, especially since they had so little to go on right now.

"Thanks," Egan told his deputy. "I'll be working from back here a while longer. Fewer windows."

Though it hadn't been necessary to add that last part. Thea and Jordan were well aware that the gunman who'd attacked them was still at large, and Egan's office was just off the squad room, where Jordan could be an easier target for a sniper.

"I understand. I'll let you know when the marshal arrives," Thea added before she ended the call.

"The marshal?" Jordan immediately asked.

"I put in that safe house request. There's a place near here, and a marshal's checking it out now."

Jordan nodded and sipped her coffee, but Egan noticed that wasn't exactly a happy look she was sporting. "You don't think the safe house is a good idea?" But he didn't wait for her to answer. "Surely, you don't want to spend another night in here with me."

It was a simple comment, definitely nothing sexual, but it didn't get a simple response. Jordan's gaze came to his, and he saw the heat again. Maybe because of the whole spending-the-night-together thing. They hadn't done that in years, but the last time had been when they were still lovers. And he darn sure hadn't slept in a chair back then. He'd been in bed with her.

The memories came. Of Jordan and him. And even though they weren't memories he especially wanted, they were better than the nightmarish ones he'd been having of Shanna.

"Yes," she muttered as if she knew exactly what he was thinking. "I think it's just a knee-jerk reaction on our parts. It's something to think about other than the fact someone tried to kill us."

Maybe she was right. Of course, the attraction had been around long before the attack, but it was best not to bring up that reminder.

"As for the safe house, yes, I think it's a good idea," she said. She paused. "You said the marshals will be guarding me."

He frowned. "You have a problem with that?"

"Maybe. Because of Christian. He has a lot of friends who are marshals. I just wondered if the one checking out the safe house is someone you can trust."

Egan had thought he could, but now he wasn't so sure. "I don't personally know the guy," he admitted. "Do you have someone in mind you'd rather me use for this?"

"No," she readily admitted. Then, she huffed. "I would say private security is the way to go, but I just don't know where the threat is coming from. If it's from Christian…"

She didn't finish that. No need. Because a well-connected cop would have friends in personal security, as well. Hell. He didn't want to hand over Jordan to someone with connections to a killer, but then he also didn't want to keep doing bodyguard duty. It was bringing back too much of the past. Still, he might not have a choice. In the short term anyway. But he might be able to call in enough reserve deputies to arrange a protection detail.

"Court managed to track down Irene Adair," Egan explained to her. "She's alive," he quickly added when he saw the renewed alarm in Jordan's eyes. "Her boyfriend's an Austin cop, and he said he'd keep an eye on her."

"Good." She took a deep breath and repeated that.

"How are your stitches?" he asked, motioning toward her shoulder. Even though she was wearing a shirt, he could still see the edge of the bandage on the front of her neck.

"It hurts," she admitted. "I'll take something if it keeps up."

He doubted that. They were both fighting to keep a clear head, which was why they were downing coffee like water. Egan finished off his cup and poured himself another one.

"There's no word yet on the truck that our attacker was driving," he said. Since they were going to be trapped in the break room for a while longer, he figured he might as well get her up to speed on the investigation. "San Antonio PD and the Rangers are helping with that."

"What about the blanket the dead woman was wrapped in? Anything unusual about that?"

Egan had to shake his head. "It was mass produced, but the lab might find some trace evidence on it. Ditto for the note. And no, the clown who wrote it hasn't called yet."

Her fingers tightened around the cup she was holding. "And what will you do when he does?"

"Talk things out with him." He choked back a groan. "Of course, that might not work, but if there is some kind of demand for cash, then I can arrange a drop so we can trap his guy."

She stayed quiet a moment, probably giving that some thought. "That sounds dangerous."

It would be, but Egan wasn't going to put too much energy into working that out right now. "The note could have been placed with the body merely to let us know that the murder was connected to us. Maybe it was even meant to scare us."

"It worked," she admitted. "I'm scared." That grip on the cup got even tighter until her knuckles were white.

Egan touched her fingers to let her know to relax, but he quickly realized that touching Jordan under any circumstances just wasn't a good idea. That little brush of his skin on hers was enough to send the coil of heat through him again, and that was why he stepped back.

His phone rang, giving him a welcome reprieve. At least it was welcome until he glanced at the screen and didn't recognize the number. His heartbeat kicked up a notch, and he put the call on speaker and hit the app to record it just in case this was from the would-be killer.

It wasn't.

"I'm Detective Martinez from San Antonio PD," the caller said when Egan answered and identified himself. "My lieutenant said you wanted us to keep you updated on Tori Judd."

"I did. Did you find her?"

"No. There's still no sign of her, and she hasn't checked in with her parents or the law office where she works. We're at her house right now, though. Her folks had a spare key, and they came over to let us in so we could have a look around." He paused. "And we might have found something."

Egan wanted to curse because he was betting that something wasn't good. Rather than speculate about how bad it could be, he just waited for the detective to continue.

"There doesn't seem to be signs of a struggle in her house," Martinez explained. "No busted locks or indications of forced entry, but there was a letter in the trash can next to her desk. That's why I'm calling. The letter mentions you, Sheriff McCall."

"I've never met Tori." That didn't mean she didn't know who he was, though. It was possible Tori had found out about Shanna, and if so, the newspaper articles about her murder had mentioned Egan. "Did Tori write the letter?"

"No. The return address says it's from the Gift of Life Foundation."

Jordan pulled in her breath. "That's a group for organ recipients. They can write letters to the families of the donors to thank them, and the families can write back through the Gift of Life. That way, the names and addresses of the donors' families and the recipients are kept secret."

"Well, it doesn't appear the person who wrote this letter kept his name a secret. It seems to be a reply to Tori's letter to thank him for the heart she got. It's short, only a couple of lines, but the language is pretty raw," Martinez added. "You want me to read it to you or would you rather I send you a photo of it?"

"Read it but leave out the language. I can fill in the blanks."

"All right. Here goes. 'Don't send me another letter to go on and on about how thankful you are for getting something you shouldn't have. I don't even want you alive when my precious girl is dead. As far as I'm concerned, you helped kill her. You, Jordan Gentry and Egan McCall.' The person who wrote the letter signed it Leeroy Sullivan. Does that name mean anything to you?"

Egan cursed, probably using some of the words that Martinez had omitted. "Yeah, and I'll get him in for questioning ASAP. But just in case the letter is a fake, I want it processed for prints."

"Sure. Will do."

"You said the letter was in the trash?" Egan pressed.

"Yes. It was a little hard to read because it had a couple of cuts and gashes on the paper. You know, like maybe somebody had stabbed it with a knife."

Jordan made a soft sound. A quick intake of breath. And she looked pale again. Without letting go of his phone, he took hold of her arm and had her sit back down on the sofa.

"There's no knife nearby, though," the detective went on. "And she didn't report the letter to the cops even though it does sound threatening to me."

It did to Egan, as well. He didn't know Tori, but it was possible the woman ripped up the letter if it'd upset her. That was about the best angle Egan could come up with for this. The other angle was that Leeroy had found her address and gone there to take out his rage on an innocent woman who just happened to have his daughter's heart.

"If Tori turns up or if we find anything else, I'll give you a call," Martinez assured him before he ended the call.

Egan turned off the recorder function and was about to call Leeroy, but there was a knock at the door. A moment later, Thea opened it and stuck her head inside.

"There's someone here to see you," she said. But Thea wasn't looking at Egan. Her attention was on Jordan. "He's a cop. And he says he's got proof of who's trying to kill you."

Chapter Six

"A cop," Jordan repeated under her breath. She was about to ask his name, but it wasn't necessary because she heard the too-familiar voice in the squad room when he called out for her.

Christian.

Great. She wasn't anywhere near the right frame of mind to see him, but he certainly knew how to get her attention. *He says he's got proof of who's trying to kill you.* And maybe he did. But getting that so-called proof wouldn't be a pleasant experience. Maybe not a safe one, either.

Of course, Christian wasn't the only one who seemed unsafe at the moment. After hearing about the ripped-up letter in Tori's house, Leeroy was certainly a suspect. Then again, he'd never made his anger a secret, and perhaps someone had planted the letter to frame him. Maybe someone like Kirk or Christian.

"Jordan, you need to see me now," Christian demanded. "It's important." He sounded close. And he was. That was because he'd obviously followed Thea down the hall to the break room.

Thea stepped in front of Christian, blocking him from entering, and Egan moved in front of Jordan. Obviously, he considered Christian a threat because Egan put his hand over his gun.

Since Christian was a head taller than Thea, he had no trouble seeing Egan and her. He also made a sweeping glance around the break room, his gaze lingering for a moment on the covers on the sofa and then on her hair that was still damp from her shower. His expression changed just enough to let her know that he was filling in the blanks. However, he wasn't filling them in correctly because he seemed to believe that Egan and she had had sex.

"I wondered where you'd stayed the night," Christian grumbled, and he shifted back to Egan. "I guess you no longer believe the sheriff is trying to kill you if you spent the night with him."

No, she didn't think Egan was a would-be killer, but Christian's tone troubled her. It sounded as if he was mocking her for believing it in the first place.

"I guess you no longer believe that I made up the threat," she fired back. "After all, you told Deputy Morris that you had proof of who was trying to kill me."

"That's proof I'll want to see," Egan insisted.

Christian certainly didn't jump to agree with Egan's demand, and he looked as if he was having a debate with himself about that. However, he must have known if he truly did have evidence that he would have to share it with Egan. After all, the attack had not only happened in Egan's jurisdiction, but he'd also nearly been killed by the gunman.

"Fine," Christian spat out like profanity. "Let's go to your office where we can talk."

Now it was Egan's turn to hesitate, and he finally shook his head. "We'll use one of the interview rooms. No windows," he added to her under his breath.

Jordan watched Christian to see if he was

unhappy about that, but he didn't have a reaction. He merely followed them into the hall. The other deputy, Ian, was there, and he had his hand over his holstered gun as if he expected some kind of trouble.

"You want me to stay with you?" Thea asked Egan. "To take notes or something?" What the deputy was probably asking was if her boss wanted some backup. It was a good offer because it was possible there was just as much threat inside the building as there was from a potential sniper at the window.

Egan shook his head. "Go ahead and call Court, though, and see if he has any updates. Also press to get those dental records."

Thea nodded and cast another uneasy glance at Christian before she went back in the direction of the squad room.

"Dental records," Christian repeated. "You're trying to confirm that Tori Judd is the dead woman."

Egan ignored that comment, probably because he didn't want to share any info about the case with Christian. "What evidence do you have?"

That tightened Christian's jaw a little.

"We're on the same side, Sheriff. I want Jordan to be safe just as much as you do."

She hoped that was true, but Egan certainly didn't look as if he believed it. He huffed and stared at Christian, obviously waiting for the cop to tell them what he'd learned.

Christian finally huffed, too, and took out a piece of paper from his pocket. If it was indeed evidence, it wasn't much because there was only a name written on the paper.

Leon Brunson.

Jordan repeated the name a couple of times, but it didn't mean anything to her. "Who is he?" she asked.

"A criminal informant. A good one, too. After I found out about the truck used in last night's attack, I started asking around."

Egan didn't ask how Christian had heard about the truck. He'd learned about it through police channels. "And?" Egan prompted when Christian didn't continue.

"Leon Brunson knew about a chop shop. One that also does custom builds from stolen auto parts. He said he was at the shop earlier in the week, and he saw a blue truck that the owners had just finished building. Don't bother calling about it," Christian added to

Egan when he took out his phone. "The shop is no longer there. When I started asking questions, it picked up and moved."

Now Egan cursed. "Then, you shouldn't have been asking questions until I'd had a chance to check it out."

Christian's eyes narrowed. "Don't tell me how to do my job. I've been a cop just as long as you have, and I've had a lot of experience dealing with things like this. I knew I had a very narrow window of time to get any info from the shop."

"A window of time that you could have told me about," Egan argued.

Christian's glare only got worse. "Those men wouldn't have talked to some cowboy cop from a hick town."

Egan stared at him. "Apparently, they didn't talk to you, either, if they closed up shop."

Bingo. That really didn't help Christian's stare. "Do you want to hear what I learned from Leon or not?"

"I'm all ears." And there was plenty of sarcasm in Egan's voice.

"Leon said he was there when the buyer picked up the truck," Christian answered once he got his jaw unclenched. "He gave me a description of the guy, and it sounded familiar so I showed him two pictures. One of Leeroy Sullivan and the other of Kirk Paxton. He said it was Kirk."

Jordan pulled back her shoulders. "He was certain?"

"Certain enough."

She had no idea what that meant, especially since the info had come from a criminal informant. One Christian had almost certainly paid for the info. And it was also possible that someone else, maybe Leeroy, had perhaps hired the man to lie to Christian so that they in turn would believe that Kirk had been the one responsible for the attack.

"I'll have a Texas Ranger talk to Leon," Egan said, letting Christian know he wasn't just going to take his word for this. "And I'll have my deputy get Kirk in here for questioning." Egan did that by firing off a text to Thea.

"I want to be here when you interview Kirk," Christian insisted.

Egan shook his head. "If I learn anything that falls into your jurisdiction, I'll let you know." He paused for only a few seconds. "And now why don't you tell me your reason for visiting Leeroy Sullivan."

Yes, that was something she wanted to know, as well. "I'd especially like for you to explain why you told Leeroy that you thought I was crazy," Jordan added.

Christian didn't curse exactly, but that was what it looked as if he wanted to do. "Really? Now you're questioning my motive about that?" He grumbled something else under his breath that she didn't catch. "I saw Leeroy because I wanted to find out if he was connected to the deaths of those other two women, Breanna Culver and Cordell Minter. He didn't admit to anything, but I believe he could be a loose cannon."

Jordan believed that, too, but it didn't explain the part about Christian claiming she was crazy so she motioned for him to continue.

Christian took in a long breath before he started talking again. "It was obvious that Leeroy doesn't like you or Egan so I thought if I fed him something he wanted to hear, that he would open up. I wanted to make him believe we were of a like mind, and that in turn would get him to trust me. It didn't work, by the way. He just kept spouting his hatred for you two and his grief over losing his daughter." He paused. "I believe Leeroy could be a very dangerous man."

Again, Jordan thought that, too, but what they needed was something more than talk and a shredded letter.

"It wasn't your place to visit a person of interest in what could be three murders," Egan said to Christian. His tone had warning written all over it. "Why have you taken such a strong interest in this case?"

Christian kept his stare on Egan for a moment before he turned to Jordan. "You know why," he said to her. "I care for you. Maybe more than care," he added in a frustrated-sounding grumble. "And I know you don't feel the same, but that doesn't change how things are for me."

Jordan wasn't exactly shocked about Christian's feelings, but she hadn't expected him to spell them out like that. Especially not in front of Egan.

Egan looked at her, no doubt to see her reaction. She shook her head and aimed her answer at Christian. "I don't want you to have feelings for me. And I need you to back off of this investigation."

Christian looked as if she'd slapped him.

"You're in danger, Jordan. I'm trying to stop someone from killing you."

"I'm well aware of that, but you're not helping me right now. I need you to do as Egan said and back off."

Christian sighed, put his hands on his hips and volleyed a few glances at both Egan and her. "Fine. But I'm a hundred percent sure you'll regret this."

Egan moved in front of her again. No doubt because that sounded like a threat. But Christian didn't add anything else. He gave them both a final glance and walked out. Jordan wished that meant she was seeing the last of him, but she wondered if Christian would indeed stop interfering in the investigation.

"You knew he was in love with you?" Egan asked. He stepped into the doorway and watched the man leave.

"Yes." But then Jordan had to shake her head. "I know that he claims to care for me."

That sent Egan's gaze shifting to her. "You think it's all an act?"

"I just don't know," she admitted. "We've spent a lot of time together going over those old cases. He's always been, well, attentive.

And he's asked me out a few times. I wasn't interested," she added.

Egan opened his mouth as if to ask a question, but he seemed to change his mind about what he was going to say. Maybe he didn't want to hear her admit the reason she hadn't dated Christian was because of him. Because she still had feelings for Egan. It wasn't especially something Jordan wanted to admit to him, either, but she was afraid it was true.

"I've always had an uneasy feeling about Christian," she added. And it was the truth.

"Because of those case files." Egan made a sound of frustration, snatched up the piece of paper with Leon's name on it and headed back toward the break room.

Jordan followed him, and once he was there, he immediately picked up his laptop and opened the death penalty files that she had been reviewing for her job.

"You said there were two cases you were suspicious about," Egan reminded her. And those were the two that he pulled up onto the screen.

Egan began to read through them, but there was no need for Jordan to do that. She'd studied them in such depth that the details were all still fresh in her mind.

"As I told you, Christian was the arresting officer in both cases. They happened nearly two years apart, but both involved human trafficking that had resulted in the deaths of several women. One of the victims was just a teenager. Both were big-money operations, and the two men arrested were middlemen."

That obviously got Egan's attention because he looked up at her. "Were the bosses ever caught?"

She had to shake her head. "If they were, they weren't specifically connected to these two cases."

Egan stayed quiet a moment while he continued to read the files. "How were the two middlemen caught?"

"The cops were tipped off, and in both cases the chain of evidence led directly to the two men who were arrested."

"Men who Christian arrested," he grumbled under his breath.

Obviously, Egan was suspicious. Jordan was, too. But there was something else that stood out about these two cases. "Both men arrested were on parole for other violations, and Shanna was their parole officer."

Egan's head whipped up, their eyes connecting, but he didn't say anything for several long moments. "What's the timing of the men's arrests and Shanna's murder?"

"The first arrest was two years before Shanna's death. The second one happened the same month."

A muscle tightened in Egan's jaw. "It could be a coincidence," he said.

And she prayed that was true. "I've looked for anything to indicate Shanna was murdered because of either of these two men, and I haven't made any connection."

"I'll search, too," Egan assured her. "In the meantime, I think it's a good idea to stay away from Christian."

His gaze locked with hers again, and even though Jordan had no intention of arguing about what he was saying, it seemed as if Egan was waiting for her to do just that. Or at least he was waiting for something anyway. And then it hit her. This could be about the attraction again. It definitely wasn't a good time for it while they were discussing Shanna and possible motives for not only her murder but also the attack against them.

Egan looked disgusted with himself, and Jordan figured he was about to put some distance between them. However, before he could move, his phone rang, and she saw Thea's name on the screen. Since he'd asked the deputy to get him any updates on the case, Egan answered it right away, and he put the call on speaker.

"I just got a call from one of the reserve deputies," Thea immediately said. "Dakota Tillman."

Jordan knew Dakota. He'd once worked full-time for Egan but was taking a break to finish his criminal justice degree.

"They're at Kirk's place now, and they need one of us to get out there." Thea paused. "They found something."

Chapter Seven

Egan figured whatever Dakota and the other reserve deputy had found, it had to be important, so he just waited for Thea to continue. He didn't have to wait long.

"Dakota found a .38 Smith & Wesson in the bottom of Kirk's dresser drawer," Thea explained. "It was wrapped in plastic and hidden under several layers of clothes. Dakota said he was pretty sure it had been recently fired, and there appear to be traces of blood on it."

Jordan obviously realized the importance of that because she pulled in a hard breath. Their still yet-to-be-identified Jane Doe had been killed with a .38.

"What did Kirk have to say about this?" Egan asked. Because he wanted to know how the man was going to try to explain the hidden gun.

"Kirk isn't at the house," Thea went on. "He's actually on his way here, but his live-in housekeeper is there, and she's putting up a fuss about the deputies taking the weapon."

"We have a search warrant," Egan reminded her, though he was sure it wasn't necessary. Thea knew that, and the deputies had almost certainly shown the housekeeper the warrant when they entered the house.

"Yes, but she ran into the backyard with it, and she's threatening to throw it in the pool. She said that Kirk told her that the cops were trying to frame him and that she believes they planted the gun."

Well, hell. Jordan looked as if she wanted to curse the same words that Egan had just belted out.

"Call Court and tell him to go to the scene to assist you," Egan instructed. "I want the housekeeper arrested and that .38 taken to the lab ASAP." He would have preferred to go there himself, but it was too risky to take Jordan. Too risky to leave her at the station, as well.

"Kirk is on his way here," Jordan repeated when Egan had finished his call with Thea.

Yes, because Egan had wanted to question him about the chop shop allegation that Christian had made, but now he could ask Kirk about the gun, too. But he understood the concern he heard in Jordan's voice. Kirk was a hothead under normal circumstances, and his housekeeper had likely told him about the reserve deputies and the gun. That meant Kirk was going to be even more unpleasant than usual.

"You can wait here or in my office when I question him," Egan said.

She nodded, but that wasn't a look of agreement in her eyes. "If Kirk truly did try to kill us, I'd like to hear what he has to say. I won't compromise the interview," she quickly added. "I just want to listen."

Her nerves were already right there at the surface, and Egan knew that it wouldn't help her to hear what would almost certainly be another Kirk tirade, but he couldn't refuse. Because she was right. If Kirk was the one who was after them, then she might be able to pick up on something when Egan questioned him.

Egan's phone rang again, and he braced himself in case it was one of the reserve deputies calling to tell him that things had escalated in a bad way at Kirk's house. But it wasn't. However, the name that popped up on a screen was a familiar one. Harlan McKinney, the marshal who was setting up the safe house for Jordan. It certainly wasn't something Egan had forgotten about, but with everything else going on, he'd put it on the back burner.

"Sheriff McCall," Harlan greeted the moment Egan answered. Since this was likely about Jordan, he put the call on speaker. "I have a problem. I believe the location of the safe house might have been compromised."

That brought back the knot in Egan's stomach. "What happened?"

"Nothing yet, but it's possible someone hacked into the computer system. There's been some sort of irregular activity, and even though I don't know for sure, someone might have been able to get access to info on the safe house we were setting up for Jordan Gentry."

Egan heard the hitch in Jordan's breath and saw the renewed fear in her eyes. "Who did this?" Her voice barely had any sound, but the marshal must have heard her anyway because he answered.

"I'm guessing you're Miss Gentry?" the marshal asked, and he didn't continue until

Jordan had confirmed that she was. "I don't know who could have done the hacking, but trust me, if there's been a breach, I'll find out who's responsible. In the meantime, I don't want you anywhere near that safe house."

Egan didn't want her there, either, but that left him with a huge problem. He needed a place to take her where the would-be killer couldn't get to her.

"I can put in another request for a second safe house," McKinney went on, "but I'd rather not do that until I'm sure the problem has been fixed."

"I understand," Egan answered. "I'll make my own arrangements for Jordan." Though at the moment he wasn't sure what those would be.

"Just be careful," the marshal warned him. "If someone can hack our system, they can probably hack yours, too." And with that stomach-knotting reminder, he ended the call.

"I don't think Christian has hacking skills," Jordan immediately said. "What about Kirk or Leeroy?"

Egan had to shake his head. "If they're good at that sort of thing, they haven't spread that news around. But it's possible one of them hired a hacker. Christian could have done that, too."

A thin weary breath left her mouth. "In other words, this doesn't rule out any of our suspects."

No, and the not knowing was clearly taking a toll on Jordan. Of course, the lack of sleep wasn't helping, either. It would have been too much for most people to handle, but he wasn't even sure that Jordan was in good health. And speaking of health, Jordan no longer looked steady.

"Are you okay?" he asked. "Do you need your meds?"

"It's not time for my next dose," she assured him.

"What about pain meds? Those stitches and your head are probably hurting."

"I'm fine."

She wasn't *fine*. Far from it, and he only hoped her stark expression was from the head injury and that it wasn't some symptom caused by the transplant. Egan took hold of her arm, intending to have her sit down on the sofa. But at the exact moment he touched her, Jordan looked up at him.

Definitely not good.

Because just like that, the old attraction re-turned, and now it was mixed with the other feelings he was having for her. The need to do his job and protect her.

"Yes," she said. "I'm sorry about this."

He knew exactly what she meant, but Egan didn't confirm it. Not with words anyway. However, he did do something pretty darn stupid. With his hand still clutching her wrist, he pulled her closer until she was in his arms.

She made another sound. Not a weary sigh this time. This was more of relief, and she seemed to melt against him. Worse, Egan felt himself melt a little, too. The memories came flooding back. Memories of the times she'd been his lover, and even though he tried to push those images away, he failed. The heat just washed over him until he thought about doing something stupid.

Like kissing her.

Even after all these years Egan thought he could remember the taste of her. The way she would feel if he pressed his mouth to hers.

"You'd regret it," he heard her whisper.

True. And Jordan would regret it as well, because they didn't just have memories of the attraction. There were those of Shanna's murder, and they would no doubt come flooding back if he opened this particular door with Jordan.

She was the one who moved away from him, stepping back until they were no longer touching. The corner of her mouth lifted into a smile. "At least we're not at each other's throats. That's progress."

No. It wasn't. Because it was easier for him to deal with the anger than with the grief. Or the heat. Thankfully, though, Egan didn't have to face either at the moment because he heard a familiar voice coming from the squad room.

Kirk.

Good. Even though he wasn't looking forward to dealing with the man, it would get his mind back on business. Besides, Kirk could maybe give them the answers they needed to blow this investigation wide open.

Egan gathered his breath and made his way to the squad room. As expected, Thea was there, and she was frisking the man. Something that obviously didn't please Kirk, but Egan didn't care. He didn't want an armed suspect in the building.

Like the other times that Egan had seen Kirk, he was dressed like a cowboy. A rich one. Which he was. As a cattle broker, Kirk made plenty of money, and from what Egan had heard, he spent plenty of it, too. He had a reputation for womanizing and throwing expensive parties. Oh, and hiring lawyers to help overturn his brother's conviction.

Ian had gotten up from his desk, and he seemed to be standing guard while Thea patted down Kirk. Good. With three lawmen and a former cop in the building, maybe Kirk would think twice before starting any trouble.

Kirk looked past her, his attention on Egan. "I just got off the phone with my housekeeper."

"I hope you told her to surrender that gun," Egan growled.

"I did, but you know that's a plant. It's not mine. One of your deputies put that gun in my house."

"I know no such thing. But the lab should be able to tell us something. For instance, if your prints are on the .38 and if the blood on it belongs to a woman who was murdered. A woman we've yet to identify."

"And if it is her blood, it proves nothing. The gun was planted."

Maybe. But Egan wasn't going to give him

the benefit of the doubt just yet. He motioned for Kirk to follow him to the interview room, but the man didn't budge even when Thea moved away from him.

"My lawyer's on the way," Kirk snapped. "You're not starting an interrogation until she gets here."

Great. He'd lawyered up. Of course, that was probably a smart move, considering the gun found at his house, but it meant Egan was going to have to hold off on getting those answers.

Or not.

"I know what you're trying to do," Kirk continued, shifting his attention to Jordan. "You're trying to set me up to protect your cop friend."

"Christian?" she asked. And it was definitely a question. Jordan shook her head. "Why would I protect him?"

"Because you're best pals. Probably lovers, too. All of this is starting to get messy, and you don't want him behind bars."

She huffed, folded her arms over her chest. "What do you think Christian has done that would require me to cover for him by framing you?"

Kirk opened his mouth as if to answer, but Egan lifted his hand to stop him. While he wanted to hear what Kirk had to say about that, he needed to do something first. Egan read the man his rights. Since part of that included the mention of his attorney, Egan thought it might be a reminder for Kirk to shut up. But no. Kirk just kept on talking.

"I figure Christian's a dirty cop, just like you were. And like you are now." Kirk aimed a glare at Egan.

"I'll bite. How am I dirty?" Egan asked. "Because you can't possibly think I did anything to put your brother behind bars."

"No, but this is about the vendetta that Jordan and you are carrying on. You don't want me around because you think I might get someone to hear the truth—that Drew wasn't mentally stable the night he pulled the trigger. He should be in a hospital, not on death row."

"A jury didn't see it that way," Jordan pointed out. "I didn't see it that way, either."

"Yeah, you were a dirty cop who likely set him up. I figure you wanted Shanna out of the way so you could be with your lover-boy here, and you and Christian used my brother to take Shanna out of the picture."

The anger roared through Egan, and it took every ounce of willpower not to punch the guy. He reminded himself that Kirk almost certainly wanted him to throw a punch because it would then in turn compromise the investigation.

"Of course, your plan didn't work," Kirk continued. "Because Egan and you still aren't together. Maybe his guilty conscience got the best of him and he figured out you're bad news."

"Shanna was my friend," Jordan said, her words barely louder than a whisper. "I wouldn't have knowingly put her in the path of a killer."

Unlike Egan, she didn't seem to be having trouble with the anger that Kirk had just provoked. But her eyes shimmered as she fought back tears. Kirk certainly wasn't on the verge of tears, though. The man had a smug look on his face because he was well aware that he'd just hit a very raw nerve with Jordan.

Egan considered returning verbal fire by reminding Kirk that he had just spelled out his motive for why he would want Jordan and him dead. But it was best to keep that until the lawyer was present, and then Egan could fully question him about it.

Thea's phone dinged with a text message, and the moment she read it, she looked at Egan. "The deputies got the gun from the housekeeper. They're arresting her for obstruction of justice and sending the gun to the lab."

Good on both counts, but the news only made Kirk's eyes narrow even more. Then he cursed. "Leeroy," he ground out "He came to my house last night, and he could have planted the gun then."

Interesting. "Now you're saying it's Leeroy who was behind the attacks. Just a few seconds ago, you were blaming Jordan and me. It seems as if you're having trouble making up your mind."

Kirk made a sound of raw frustration. "I didn't say that Leeroy was a saint. He hates me because of my brother."

"And yet he paid you a visit," Egan pointed out.

Kirk suddenly got quiet, and for several moments Egan thought that maybe this would be the end of their little chat, but then Kirk shook his head. "He's never done that before, and that's why I should have known something was up. He said he wanted to talk to me about the women who'd been killed. The ones who got Shanna's organs."

Jordan and Egan exchanged a glance, and even though she didn't say anything, Egan knew that had caught her attention as much as it had his. Still, Egan didn't want to question him about it because it could be argued that Egan had continued an interrogation after Kirk had lawyered up.

"Leeroy must have planted the gun when he came to my house," Kirk added a moment later. "He asked to use the bathroom, and he could have done it then. It's definitely not mine. I don't own a .38."

"He doesn't have one registered to his name," Thea explained. "I checked."

Yeah, but that didn't mean Kirk hadn't bought it illegally. Of course, it was just as possible that Leeroy had indeed set him up. And if so, then Egan was going to have to untangle this mess to get to the truth.

"Why would Leeroy do something like this now?" Jordan asked Kirk, but she immediately waved off the question. Probably because she, too, remembered that asking questions wasn't a good idea without Kirk's lawyer present.

Kirk ignored her waving-off gesture, though, because he turned to her. However, he didn't jump into an answer. Instead, he glanced out the window when a car pulled to a stop in front of the building and a woman stepped out. "Maybe because of her." He tipped his head toward their visitor, who was now making her way to the door. "That's my lawyer, and Leeroy probably heard about it."

Of all the things that Egan had thought Kirk might say, that wasn't one of them. And this was something he could most certainly ask and not violate any protocols of an interrogation. "Who's your lawyer?"

Kirk gave them a blank look as if the answer were obvious. But he was giving that blank look to Jordan. "I thought you knew."

Jordan shook her head. "Knew what?"

The corner of Kirk's mouth lifted into a slight smile. Not a good smile, either. And he turned toward the woman who walked in. It wasn't someone Egan knew personally, but he certainly recognized her from the photos.

The same woman who'd received Shanna's heart.

Tori Judd.

Chapter Eight

Jordan heard the small gasp of surprise that she made, but the feelings inside her were far from small. The first thing she felt was relief.

The woman hadn't been murdered after all.

But the questions soon followed the relief. Yes, Tori was alive, but then who was their Jane Doe?

"Tori Judd?" Egan questioned.

The lawyer nodded, confirming that. Though Jordan hadn't needed confirmation. Tori looked exactly like her DMV photo. The same long auburn hair and intense blue eyes.

"We've been looking for you," Egan said to the woman. "Because we thought you were dead."

"Yes. I just heard about that on the drive over." She touched her fingers to her forehead. "I've been dealing with a migraine for the past two days so I turned off my phone and took enough meds to knock me out. I didn't see all the calls until I was on the way over here. I got in touch with my parents to let them know I was okay, but I figured I could wait and tell you in person."

Jordan glanced at Egan to see if he was buying this, but she couldn't tell. She certainly had her doubts. "You weren't at your house," Jordan told her.

"No," Tori answered at the same moment that Kirk said, "She was staying at my place."

Neither Tori nor Kirk added anything to that, but after seeing the look they gave each other, Jordan was even more confused. It was the sort of look that passed between lovers.

"You two are together," Egan grumbled. And Jordan heard the skepticism and disgust in his voice. "You do know that Kirk is trying to get Shanna's killer released from jail."

Tori nodded again. "I doubt this will make sense to you. Or you," she added to Jordan. "I know from everything I learned that you both loved Shanna, but Kirk isn't responsible for her death. He's just trying to be a good brother."

Egan mumbled some profanity. "There's a

difference of opinion about that, but let's agree to disagree on that specific point. But there's something you can't dispute. Someone murdered a woman who looks like you. What do you know about that?"

"Nothing," Tori said without hesitation. "But from what Kirk told me, you believe he committed the crime. He didn't. He was at his house with me."

"While you were *knocked out* on pain meds," Egan fired back. He didn't need to spell out that she was either lying about the migraine or there was no way she could have known if Kirk had murdered the woman or not.

But who the heck was the woman?

"When the San Antonio cops searched your house, they found a letter," Jordan said. "One from the Gift of Life Foundation."

"It was shredded," Egan added.

Until Egan had said that last part, Tori had had no reaction. But she had a reaction now. Her eyes widened, and she no longer looked as confident or as steady as she had when she'd arrived.

"That letter upset me a lot so I ripped it

up." Her voice was a little shaky, too. "Leeroy seemed, well, crazy, and I was afraid of him."

"That's why she's been staying with me," Kirk volunteered.

Strange since Kirk might have been the one who was following her. Of course, it was just as likely that it was Leeroy.

"Now you can see why I was so concerned when Leeroy showed up at my place," Kirk went on. "I thought he was there to find Tori, but he never even brought up her name."

Egan stayed quiet a moment as if processing that, and he turned back to Tori. "You do know that two recipients of Shanna's organs are dead?"

She nodded. "I figured that out after I got the letter from Leeroy." She tightened her grip on her purse. "Someone wants to kill me, don't they?"

"I believe someone does. Jordan, too." Egan motioned to the bandage on Jordan's head. "The person nearly succeeded with Jordan. My advice would be for you to go into protective custody."

A burst of air left Kirk's mouth. A laugh,

sort of, but it wasn't from humor. "Why should Tori trust you to keep her safe?"

Egan gave him a look that could have frozen the desert, and he tapped his badge. "But I didn't say *my* protective custody. She can call the rangers or marshals."

"You really think that's necessary?" Kirk asked.

Egan lifted his shoulder. "Two other organ recipients are dead. So is another woman who's connected to this in some way. And someone tried to kill Jordan. I think that's a good indication that Tori might be in danger."

"But you're not positive the attack and those deaths actually had anything to do with Shanna," Kirk argued.

"No, but common sense tells me Tori should be taking precautions."

"I will," the lawyer assured him, interrupting whatever else it was that Kirk had been about to say.

At least Tori seemed to be understanding the seriousness of all of this. Well, maybe. It was just as possible that she was so mixed up with Kirk that he'd been able to convince her that she wasn't in any real danger.

"What about the other recipient, Irene Adair?" Tori asked.

"She's alive, as far as we know," Jordan answered.

"So, is Kirk free to go?" Tori asked after a crisp nod.

"No." And Egan didn't hesitate for even a second. "In addition to the gun and the murdered woman, I need to ask him about a chop shop in San Antonio. I have a witness who identified him as being there."

Kirk lifted his shoulder. "The mechanic who comes to my house to service all my vehicles lives in San Antonio. But if he's got a connection to a chop shop, this is the first I'm hearing about it. Who's the witness?"

"Someone credible," Egan growled.

That could be an out-and-out lie, but at the moment, Jordan was going to accept it as truth. Apparently, so was Egan. Or at least he was going to let Kirk believe he believed it.

Kirk clearly didn't accept it, though. His mouth tightened. "I'm guessing this is just another thing you'll try to use to railroad me. Well, it won't work. I haven't done anything illegal."

Again, that could be a lie, but the bottom

line was, the word of a criminal informant alone wasn't enough to hold Kirk. But maybe Egan could get something off the gun.

"Take Kirk and his lawyer to the interview room," Egan instructed Thea, and he waited for her to do that before he made a call to Court.

"I was so sure Tori had been killed," Jordan said while they waited for Court to answer.

"So was I," he assured her.

And the fact that Tori was alive meant the murder and the attack might not be connected to Shanna or Drew after all. Or maybe someone just wanted it to look that way.

"Our Jane Doe isn't Tori Judd," Egan told his brother the moment that Court came on the line. Egan also put the call on speaker.

"Yeah, I just found out and was about to call you. We got an ID on the dead woman, and her name is Lorena Lovett."

The name didn't mean anything to Jordan, and judging from Egan's head shake, he didn't recognize it, either.

"Lorena was a legal assistant at a firm in Austin," Court continued. "No priors. No red flags to indicate she was involved in anything illegal. She was reported missing two days ago, and her fiancé just viewed the body and made a positive ID." He paused. "How'd you know it wasn't Tori?"

"Because she's here at the sheriff's office," Egan answered. "And get this—she's Kirk's lawyer."

Court cursed. "How the hell did that happen?"

"I'm about to find out when I interview them."

"You really think that's a good idea? I mean, because of Shanna. Dealing with Kirk alone is bad enough, but he could use this to dredge up some rough memories for you."

Jordan didn't have to guess how Egan felt about this. The memories were already there, but Court was right. Kirk could use Tori to try to push some of Egan's hot buttons, and since his patience level was probably about as low as it could get, Egan could end up saying something that would hurt this investigation.

"By any chance did Lorena work for the same law firm as Tori?" Jordan asked Court.

"No," he answered. "Tori's law firm is in San Antonio."

That didn't mean the women hadn't known each other, though, or that maybe they'd once worked together, and that might be a critical connection. Perhaps this Lorena had learned something, maybe something about Kirk, and he had her killed for it.

"The gun we got from Kirk's housekeeper is on the way to the lab," Court went on a few seconds later. "It'll be a while before we hear anything on that, and I'm guessing Kirk will say it was planted."

"Yep," Egan verified. "He said it was Leeroy, that he went to Kirk's house last night."

Court made a sound of skepticism, and Jordan felt the same way. There was something unsettling about how all of this was playing out.

"I was about to call to get Leeroy in for questioning," Egan explained.

"I can do that. I'm on my way back now. My advice—why don't you go ahead and get Jordan out of there?"

"There was a problem with the safe house," Egan explained.

"I wasn't going to suggest you take her there anyway. Dad's alone at the ranch. He moved back into the main house."

Since their father, Warren, was a former sheriff, his being alone normally wouldn't have caused that kind of alarm in Court's voice. But Jordan knew that Warren was still recovering from a gunshot wound that he'd gotten several months earlier.

"Isn't your housekeeper, Ruby, with him?" Jordan asked. Ruby had been working for the McCalls for so long that she was practically family. And even though she was in her sixties now, Jordan knew the woman could handle a firearm.

"No. Dad insisted she take some time off."

Court didn't mention his mother, but Jordan knew that the woman was in a mental hospital. She'd had a breakdown after learning about her husband's longtime affair with Alma Lawton. But even though their parents and sister weren't at the ranch, that left one other person.

"What about your wife, Rayna?" she pressed.

"She's with Rachel, and I'll have her stay there until things settle down. If you don't want to stay at the main house with Dad, you can go to the guesthouse. No one's using it now, and it has a security system."

She knew exactly what guesthouse he meant because Egan had taken her there a couple of times when they'd still been together. It wasn't ideal, but it was probably safer than a hotel.

Thea came back into the squad room, and she gave Egan a thumbs-up to indicate she had Kirk and Tori in the interview room.

"If Jordan and you go to the ranch, it'd solve two problems," Court pressed. "Dad would have someone close by to keep an eye on him. But it would also get Jordan out of the squad room and away from our suspects. I figure she's already had enough of all of them."

Jordan had indeed had *enough*, and she did want to make sure Warren was okay, but if they stayed at the sheriff's office, she might be able to learn something from the interviews. Though the chances were slim. Tori probably wasn't going to let Kirk say anything stupid or incriminating. Leeroy might let his temper get the best of him and blurt out something, but even that was a long shot.

"You're sure you want to tackle questioning both Kirk and Leeroy?" Egan asked his brother.

"Definitely. This wouldn't be nearly as hard for me to do as it would be for you. And while I'm talking to our suspects," Court went on, "Jordan and you can work on following up with the lab on the gun and trying to figure out how Lorena Lovett fits into all of this."

Egan still wasn't jumping to agree to that. But then he looked at her, and she saw his expression change. That was probably because she made the mistake of touching the bandage on her shoulder. Yes, the stitches were hurting, and she hadn't wanted to take any pain meds because it would have clouded her mind. No way could she risk that now. Still, she was in pain, and there was no way to hide that from Egan.

"How far out are you?" Egan asked Court.

"Only about fifteen minutes. Go ahead and leave. I'll be there soon enough."

Egan ended the call, but even after everything Court had just said, there was still some hesitation in Egan's eyes.

"I could follow you to the ranch," Ian volunteered. "After you're there, I could come back here if there are enough hands to help you guard the house and the rest of the grounds."

The McCall Ranch was huge, which meant it would be next to impossible to keep watch of every part of it. Egan was no doubt considering that, but after one look at her again, he nodded and then turned to Thea.

"Call one of the reserve deputies to fill in here for a while," Egan said to Thea. "If they're all tied up, ask Griff to come in."

Griff was Thea's brother, Texas Ranger Griff Morris. He would also soon be marrying Egan's sister. Better yet, he'd once been a deputy in McCall Canyon so he'd know how to handle their suspects. If Egan wanted him to handle them, that was. Apparently, he did because he motioned toward the break room.

"Get your things, and we can leave now," Egan instructed her.

Jordan nodded and headed to the break room. The interview room door was closed, but she could hear Tori and Kirk having what appeared to be a heated conversation. Jordan couldn't hear specifically what they were saying, but Tori sounded agitated. She considered putting her ear to the door, but since that would be a violation of attorney-client privilege, Jordan walked away. If Kirk was charged with something, then she didn't want to be the reason he was set free.

By the time Jordan had gotten her things and made it back to the squad room, Egan was already at the front door, and he had the cruiser keys in his hand.

"Move fast," he told her.

She did, and when they were both in the cruiser, that was when she spotted Ian in the vehicle parked directly behind them. The moment Egan pulled out, so did the deputy.

"If you're going to the ranch because of me—" she started, but Jordan didn't get a chance to finish.

"It's not just you. My dad's been getting death threats."

She pulled in a quick breath. "Because of me?"

He quickly shook his head. "We're not sure who's sending them, but he's been getting them for a couple of months now. Ever since his shooting. The threats keep getting worse with each new one he gets."

Jordan was relieved that this wasn't on her shoulders, but it couldn't be pleasant for the McCalls for this to be happening. They were a family of cowboy cops, and it probably ate away at Egan that he hadn't been able to protect his father. Warren had nearly died from his gunshot wound, and apparently someone might try again to kill him.

"My dad takes too many chances," Egan went on. He took the turn off Main Street and onto the rural road that led to the ranch. "It's almost as if he's trying to draw out the person behind the threats. Maybe so he can put an end to them. That's why Court wanted someone to be with him."

Jordan understood that need for the threats to end, and if she thought that calling out her attacker would work, then she would do it. At least then Egan might not be in danger.

"I think Kirk and Tori were arguing in the interview room," she told him.

That caused Egan to give her a long glance. "Something's not right between those two. I hope Kirk hasn't been able to convince Tori to kill the other recipients as some kind of sick revenge for his brother."

Jordan hoped that, too, but even if Tori didn't know anything about the murder plot, she could still be in danger.

"Maybe we can find something you can use to arrest Kirk," Jordan threw out there. "If Christian's CI can identify Kirk in a lineup, will that be enough for you to make an arrest?"

Egan shook his head while he continued to keep watch around them. "Just because Kirk was at the chop shop, it doesn't mean he had them build that custom truck. What I need is someone who saw Kirk with a truck like that. Maybe someone like his housekeeper."

True. But since she'd tried to keep the gun from the reserve deputies, the woman seemed very loyal to Kirk. Loyal enough to lie about a truck that was a key part of a murder investigation.

"The reserve deputies arrested the housekeeper," Egan went on, "so Court can question her, too." He added a low groan at the end of that. Probably because he was frustrated about all of these interrogation duties landing on his brother.

"I'm sorry you have to babysit me," she mumbled.

Something flashed through his eyes. Possibly anger. But Egan's attention didn't stay on her for long. That was because his phone dinged, the sound shooting through the cruiser, and when he took it from his pocket, Jordan saw his father's name on the screen. Egan immediately hit the answer button and put it on speaker.

"We have a problem," Warren McCall said

the moment he was on the line. "One of the hands just spotted an armed intruder coming over the fence."

Chapter Nine

Egan felt the slam of adrenaline and fear. This was what Court and he had been worried about.

But now he had another worry. Jordan was with him, and while everything inside him was yelling for him to get to the ranch, he could be taking her right into the middle of another attack.

"Don't even think about driving me back to the sheriff's office," she insisted. "Your father could be in danger, and you need to get there ASAP."

It wasn't a surprise that Jordan wanted him to hurry to the ranch. No way would she expect him to put her safety ahead of his father's.

And Egan didn't intend to do that.

He wanted them both safe, but that might not happen if he did indeed turn around. That would mean either heading back to the sheriff's office while Ian proceeded to the ranch. That would leave Jordan and him open for an ambush. Plus, it would leave his father more vulnerable. Ian was a deputy, but Egan might need even more backup if this intruder went after Warren.

If this guy was after him, that was.

It was entirely possible that this person was after Jordan and him. Even though Egan had told only Ian, Thea and Court that he was going to the ranch, that didn't mean the person after them hadn't anticipated what might happen. This could be a would-be killer getting himself into position to make sure Jordan and he didn't survive another attack.

Egan didn't have time to debate this with himself. "I'll be at the ranch in about five minutes," he told his father, and after he ended the call, he handed Jordan his phone. "Call Ian and tell him what's going on. Court, too." He hit the accelerator and continued toward the ranch.

Jordan made the calls while she kept watch around them. She also threw open the glove compartment. "I want a gun just in case."

He hated the idea of her having to be in a

gunfight, but there wasn't much about this situation that he liked. He reached over, his arm brushing against hers. Her muscles were already tense and knotted, something he completely understood. Egan took out the Glock that he kept as a reserve weapon and handed it to her.

"Thanks," she muttered just as his phone rang again with another call. It was his father's name on the screen again.

"Put it on speaker," Egan instructed. He wanted to hear what his dad had to say, but he also needed to keep his attention on the road. After all, the intruder could really be just a trap for another attack.

"Art lost sight of the armed man," his father immediately said.

Art Stovall was one of the top hands at the ranch and wouldn't hesitate to protect Warren. "Where did Art last see him?" Egan asked.

"The west fence near the guesthouse."

That caused Egan's chest to tighten. The guesthouse had come up during his conversation with Court. It might be just a coincidence that the intruder had gone there, but it was entirely possible that Kirk and/or Tori had heard him mention it. Even if they had, though, there probably hadn't been enough time to send someone to the ranch. Still, maybe they'd had the thug waiting nearby.

"I'm taking the final turn to the ranch now," Egan told his dad. "Stay inside and stay down."

His father made a sound to indicate that wasn't going to happen. And it wouldn't. Once a lawman, always a lawman, and there was no way his dad would just stand by and be attacked.

"I have Jordan with me," Egan added. "So when we get to the front of the house, open the door for us."

"Will do," his father assured him.

Egan motioned for Jordan to press the end-call button, and he used the remote to open the large cattle gate that stretched across the ranch road. The gate would stop someone from getting to them by vehicle, but it obviously hadn't stopped someone from coming across the fence. Egan closed it behind them as soon as Ian and they had made it through.

There were acres of pastures on each side of the road, and the ground was flat enough that it would have made it impossible for someone to hide there. It was a different story, though, when they made it to the house. The place sprawled out, and there were plenty of trees and shrubs in addition to several trucks and outbuildings. An intruder would find plenty of places to hide if he'd made it this far.

Another ranch hand, Bennie Jensen, was on the side of the house near one of the trucks. He had a rifle, which meant he'd been alerted that there was a problem. Egan wanted the hand as backup, but he didn't want him out in the open like that.

"Take cover in the barn," Egan called out to Bennie the moment he came to a stop in front of the house and opened the cruiser door. Bennie could still keep watch from there. Well, hopefully he could. No matter where he was, there'd be blind spots.

Bennie moved, hurrying to the barn, and Egan intended to hurry as well when he got Jordan from the cruiser to the house. As he'd instructed his father, the front door opened.

"Don't come out on the porch," Egan warned his dad. "Stay back."

As soon as his father had done that, Egan drew his gun and motioned for Jordan to crawl across the seat and get out on his side of the vehicle. He waited until both Ian and she had their feet on the ground before he took hold of her arm to help her get up the eight steps that led up to the porch. They got up the first two when Egan heard a sound he didn't want to hear.

A gunshot.

This one blasted through the air and slammed into the steps right where they were.

Egan got another jolt of the adrenaline, and even though he had his gun ready, he didn't know where to shoot to return fire. Plus, his first priority had to be to make sure Ian, his father and Jordan were out of the line of fire.

"Dad, get down!" Egan shouted.

Egan hooked his arm around Jordan's waist and dragged her off the steps and into the yard. It was a risk because they could still be in the path of any other bullets, but it was even riskier to try to make it to the front door. They'd be easy targets while on the steps.

They landed, hard, in the middle of some shrubs, and Egan tried not to react to the sound of pain that Jordan made. It was possible, though, that she'd been hurt in the fall. Or maybe she'd even been shot. He didn't see any blood, but he couldn't take the time to check and make sure she was okay.

That was because another bullet came at them.

This one smashed into the stone step and sent a spray of debris through the air. Egan automatically pushed Jordan all the way to the ground and covered her body with his as best he could.

"You see the shooter?" Ian called out. The deputy had scrambled beneath the cruiser. Not an ideal position, but then the bullets hadn't gone in his direction.

Egan glanced around, trying to pinpoint the direction of the two shots. They had come from straight ahead. Not from the pasture, though. He thought these shots had come from the heavily treed area on the other side of the road past the cattle gate. If so, it meant the shooter was using a long-range rifle. However, it also meant something else.

They likely had two gunmen targeting them.

Art had said he'd seen the intruder near the guesthouse. That was at the back of the main house. The guy probably wouldn't have been able to get past Bennie's or Warren's watchful eyes to make it to the front of the property. The second shooter could have already been in place by the time Jordan and he arrived at the ranch. The guy probably hadn't shot at them sooner because he would have known that the cruiser would be bullet resistant.

Egan passed Jordan his phone. "Text Ian and Dad. Tell them there could be a second gunman. Bennie needs to know that, too."

She gave a shaky nod and took his phone. That was when Egan got a better look at her. And this time he saw what he didn't want to see. Blood. The stitches on her shoulder had obviously come out, probably in the fall, and she was bleeding again. He didn't have time, though, to do anything about that because another shot came.

The third bullet was even closer than the other two had been, which told them that the shooter was adjusting his aim. He might just be able to hit them the next time. And that meant Egan had to do something now.

"Stay put," he told Jordan.

He was about to move, but she caught onto his arm. "You're not going out there," she insisted.

"I have to. I can pull the cruiser in front of you and use it to block the shots."

She was shaking her head harder with each

word he said. "You could also be killed. Whoever's doing this will gun you down."

Maybe. But he was about to tell her the
same could happen if they stayed put. At least
this way he might be able to save her from
being shot. It could save Ian and his father,
too, since his dad would almost certainly try
to return fire. In fact, he was probably already
going after his rifle. Egan would have wel-
comed that if it hadn't meant his dad would
have to come out in the open to try to stop
this.

Egan gave Jordan another warning to stay
down, but whether or not she would was anyone's guess. As a former cop, it was likely
hard for her not to give him some kind of
backup. Still, his efforts would be all for nothing if this snake managed to kill both of them.

More shots came. All of them coming way
too close to the shrubs where Jordan and he
were. When there was finally a lull, Egan took
a deep breath and launched himself toward the
cruiser. It wasn't far. Only about four yards,
but it felt like miles.

Suddenly, there was no more lull in the
shooting. The bullets came, smacking into
the ground around him as he made a dive for

the side of the cruiser. The fall hurt like the devil, but at least he was finally out of the line of fire.

Or not.

The next shot that came was from a different angle. Not on the side of the house where the barn and Bennie were. This one had come from the other side closer to Ian. Egan threw open the cruiser door just as another bullet smacked into it.

Egan looked around, trying to pinpoint this second gunman, and he saw the guy peering around the corner of the house. Since he was positive this wasn't one of the hands, Egan sent a shot his way. So did Ian. And when the guy ducked back behind cover, that gave Egan his chance to scramble into the cruiser.

The moment he was behind the wheel, Egan started the engine and pulled it in front of Jordan. At least now she was semiprotected since the porch steps would block any shots coming from the second gunman. However, that didn't mean the danger was over. The gunman in the trees must have gotten riled at Egan moving the cruiser because the shots started to come nonstop. But they were no longer going at Jordan and him.

These were going into the house.

That was when Egan saw his father in the doorway.

"Get down!" Egan shouted out to him.

Warren did drop to the floor, but Egan wasn't sure if he'd done that because of his order or if because he'd been shot.

Enough of this. With the cruiser door still open, Egan turned in the direction of the second gunman, and the moment the guy leaned out from cover, Egan fired. Not once but twice. And he put two bullets in the man's chest. He dropped, too, but Egan hoped the guy wasn't dead, just out of commission. He wanted this clown alive so he could tell them who'd put him up to doing this.

More shots cracked through the air, and it took Egan a moment to realize they weren't all coming from the first gunman. These were coming from the barn area, and for several heart-stopping moments, he thought there might be a third attacker in all of this.

But it was only Bennie.

The ranch hand had a rifle and was returning fire, his barrage of shots going in the direction of the first gunman. Since Egan didn't have a rifle, he couldn't help with that, but he could do more to protect Jordan now that the second gunman was down. He pulled even closer to her, moved to the passenger's seat and motioned for her to get in the cruiser.

She didn't waste a second doing that, and Jordan immediately took aim at the downed gunman by the side of the house. Good. With her keeping an eye on him, it freed up Egan to figure out what to do about the first shooter. He didn't want to go after him in the cruiser since it would mean taking Jordan closer to the gunfire. Too many things could go wrong with that.

Bennie continued to shoot, causing the gunman to shift his fire toward the hand. Egan hoped like the devil that Bennie got down because this guy wasn't stopping. He was either reloading very quickly or he'd brought multiple weapons with him and was trading out as soon as one was out of ammo.

There were more shots, and these caused Egan to curse. Something his father likely wanted to do as well since he was standing again and firing at the thug who was trying to kill them. Just as Egan feared, that caused the thug to turn his shots on Warren.

Hell.

Egan watched as the bullet sliced across his father's arm. It wasn't a deadly shot, but the next one could easily be. That didn't cause his father to get down, though. He kept pulling the trigger. So did Bennie.

Until finally the shooting stopped.

Egan couldn't tell if one of them had managed to take out the first gunman, but as the seconds crawled by with the silence, he figured the guy was either dead or making a run for it. He didn't mind the first possibility, but he didn't want this snake getting away. He wanted him to answer for what he'd just done.

While he kept watch around them, Egan sent Court a text to warn him that he might cross paths with this would-be killer and to have him get an ambulance out to the ranch for their dad. He was about to call Ian to tell him to head to the end of the ranch road so he could try to spot the gunman, but the movement from the corner of his eye stopped him.

"The gunman's alive," Jordan said on a rise of breath.

The gunman lifted himself up just enough, and he fired a shot right at them.

Chapter Ten

Jordan tried to keep her breathing level. She also tried not to wince in pain, but it hurt when the medic restitched her shoulder. She figured it was going to hurt a lot more when the numbing spray wore off, but that was minor in the grand scheme of things.

She'd killed a man today.

Since she'd once been a cop, Jordan had always known that doing something like that was a possibility, but still it caused her to feel raw and bruised. It didn't matter that the man she'd killed was trying to murder them. She had shot him to keep Egan, Ian, Warren, Bennie and herself alive, but it would take a while for her to feel like she'd done the right thing. Especially since a dead man couldn't give them answers.

Neither could his partner, who was still at large.

Ian had gone after him. So had Court. But they'd both come up empty. Whoever had fired the shots from those trees was long gone. Of course, that didn't mean he or she wouldn't be back to have another attempt at killing them.

The medic finished, moving to the side so he could gather up his things, and she was finally able to see Egan. He was pacing in the foyer while talking on his phone. Even though she was in the adjacent family room, she couldn't hear what he was saying. However, she could tell from his body language that he was agitated.

She turned to the other side of the room when a second medic was finishing up with Warren. He, too, was getting stitches. The bullet had grazed him, but there was an angry-looking gash on his arm. It wasn't life-threatening, but since he hadn't fully recovered from his other attack, this might set him back.

Court was next to his father, but when he saw her looking at them, he stepped away and went to her once the medic had left. "I would ask if you're okay, but I know you're not. You need a drink, meds or something?"

Jordan hadn't meant for it to happen, but at the exact moment Court was asking his question, her gaze drifted to Egan. And Court noticed, too, because the corner of his mouth lifted for a second.

"Yeah, my big brother might be a temporary fix for what you're feeling," he mumbled. Then, he sighed and scrubbed his hand over his face. "Not sure that he'd let himself get too close to you, though."

No. He wouldn't. In fact, Egan was probably cursing himself for feeling so protective of her. Those protective feelings could lead to something more. Something that he definitely wouldn't want. Jordan tried to lie to herself and say she didn't want it, either. But it was just that. A lie.

She did want Egan.

And she wasn't certain it was solely because of the spent adrenaline and tangled nerves. It had felt good earlier when he'd taken her into his arms, and she figured it would feel just as good or better now.

Jordan turned back to Court, forcing her thoughts off Egan. It wasn't the time for them, and besides, they had plenty more to discuss. Jordan started with the easy subject first.

"How's your father?" she asked.

"Not as tough as he's trying to appear to be." Court glanced back at Warren. "He's shaken up. Riled, too, that the other gunman got away."

Jordan felt the same way. Here, they'd nearly been killed again, and they still weren't any closer to figuring out who was behind this. "We won't be staying here, will we?"

Court didn't hesitate. "No. Some of the windows have been shot out, and that might have compromised the security system. Plus, we know now that a sniper can take shots at the house. I'm taking Dad to Rachel and Griff's place in town. Egan and you will go back to the sheriff's office for a little while. Just until I can finish up the interviews with Kirk and Leeroy."

With everything else going on, Jordan had forgotten about the interviews, and they were more important now than ever. Of course, she didn't expect either of the men to confess to hiring those gunmen or killing anyone, but they might slip and say something incriminating.

"Where will Egan and I go after the sheriff's office?" she pressed.

"Egan's working that out now." Court blew out a weary breath. "There's a lot that has to be worked out. We need an ID on the dead guy to see if that leads us to the person behind this. Also, a CSI team needs to process the whole area around the house and in those trees. The shooters might have left some kind of evidence behind."

That would be a good break if they had indeed done that, but Jordan wasn't counting on it. If the shooters had been pros, then they would likely have been careful about that sort of thing.

Egan finished his call and walked into the family room, glancing first at his father before making his way to her. His expression wasn't exactly pleasant, but it got even worse when he looked at the fresh bandage.

"Sorry about that," he grumbled. "I did that to you when I pushed you off the step."

"Yes, so I wouldn't be shot. Thank you. I'd rather have the stitches than a bullet in me."

That caused Court to smile a little, but when Egan saw his brother's expression, Court's smile faded, and he went back across the room to his father. When Egan's attention came back to her, their gazes connected, and she saw the stripped-down emotions there that were no doubt mirrored in her own eyes.

Since he looked ready to berate himself about allowing this attack to happen, Jordan decided to stop it with a question. An important one. "How are Ian and Bennie?" she asked. She got to her feet and tried to look a lot stronger than she felt.

"Neither was hurt."

That was good, but she figured both men would be having nightmares about this for a long time. Especially Bennie. Ian was a cop and had been trained for situations like this, but Bennie probably hadn't expected his ranch hand duties to include a shootout with hired guns.

"I'll go ahead and take Dad to Griff's," Court called out to them. "I'm guessing Jordan, Ian and you will be leaving shortly?"

Egan nodded. "After Ian finishes checking the cruisers to make sure there was no damage."

So, maybe not long at all. Jordan knew it wasn't safe to stay put, but they could also be attacked again on the road.

"I'm pretty sure I know the answer to this," Egan said, "but do you want me to take you to the hospital? The medic took care of those stitches, but—"

"No hospital. There's no reason for me to see a doctor." She hoped.

He gave her a suit-yourself nod and mumbled a "be safe" to Court and his father when they went out of the house and to the cruiser.

"Will they be okay?" Jordan asked. She followed him to the window where he watched his brother and father drive away.

Egan nodded. "Several of the hands are following them into town. Everyone will be on the lookout for that gunman who got away."

And maybe the gunman was done for the day so that Warren could get to safety. The man had been through enough. Of course, Egan and she fell into that "enough" category, too.

"This means we might end up staying in the break room again at the sheriff's office," he added a moment later.

She'd suspected as much, and while it was far from ideal, at least there'd be immediate backup around if something went wrong. It also meant, though, that Egan and she would be sharing close quarters again and therefore wouldn't get much sleep. But the close quarters wouldn't just fuel the lack of sleep. It wouldn't help the attraction, either.

Jordan looked at him, knowing it was a mistake. Because there was no way she could conceal the worry, the pain or anything else. They had just survived a horrible ordeal, and the danger might not even be over.

Egan gave a heavy sigh, reached out and pulled her into his arms. The relief was instant. With just that simple gesture, it felt as if he took some of the weariness from her body. It might have stayed as simple as relief, too, if Egan hadn't looked down at her. He growled out some profanity, but she didn't have to ask why he'd done that. That was because she saw the kiss coming before it happened.

She even felt it.

The memories of his other kisses were still plenty clear enough, but she still got a jolt when his mouth touched hers. And the heat roared through her. Jordan felt herself moving right into that kiss and closer to him. Until his chest was against her breasts. He deepened the kiss, but the sound he made wasn't one of pleasure. Egan was already regretting that he was doing this, but like her, he wasn't able to stop.

"Damn you," he whispered against her mouth.

That would have caused most women to move back, but she was positive he wasn't cursing her but rather himself. His frustration came out in the kiss, too. Almost an angry kiss. In fact, coming from any other man that was exactly what it would have been, but this was Egan. The attraction cut through anger and everything else.

For those few scalding seconds, Jordan forgot all about the attack, their past and the danger. Heck, she forgot how to think or breathe. She could only stand there and let the kiss rage on. It wasn't Egan or her who ended it. It was the sound of his phone. That must have jolted him back to reality because he finally pulled away from her.

When he took out his phone, she saw Thea's name on the screen. Since this could be important, he answered it right away and put it on speaker.

"Sorry to bother you," Thea said, "but Leeroy's yammering on about having waited around here long enough. You want me to reschedule the interview?"

"Are Tori and Kirk still there?" he asked. His breathing was still a little rushed just as hers was.

"Yes, but they're whining, too. I can reschedule them, as well."

Egan's forehead bunched up while he obviously gave that some thought. "Court will be there soon. He can talk to Tori and Kirk. Reschedule Leeroy, but put him on the phone first. I want to ask him a question."

"You're sure you're up to that after just getting shot at?" Thea pressed.

"No, I'm not sure, but put him on the phone anyway." Egan glanced out at Ian again and then motioned for her to move to the center of the room with him. Away from the windows. A reminder that the gunman could return at any moment.

A few seconds crawled by, but Leeroy finally came onto the line. "You'd better have a damn good reason for keeping me waiting," Leeroy immediately snapped. Maybe the man hadn't heard about the attack at the ranch, but it was just as likely that he didn't care. He hated Egan and her, and he wouldn't cut them any slack simply because someone had tried to kill them.

Egan didn't even respond to that. "Tell me why you visited Kirk," Egan demanded.

"You asked me that last night. Am I gonna have to explain every move I make to you now?"

"You do when you might have committed a crime." Egan huffed. "Look, my patience meter is at zero right now so either answer the question, or I'll have Thea arrest you. Why did you go to Kirk's house?"

It was hard to miss the profanity that Leeroy spat out. "Because I'm going to file a wrongful death suit against Jordan and you, and I thought I could count on Kirk as an ally."

Egan pulled back his shoulders. "A lawsuit?"

"Yeah because the two of you are partly responsible for Shanna's murder. I want both of you to pay for that."

Jordan could only sigh. Leeroy was clearly hurting over losing a child, and he apparently thought her killer's conviction wasn't enough justice. It wasn't. But nothing the man could do was going to bring Shanna back.

"So, let me get this straight," Egan said.

"You thought Kirk would help you with a lawsuit. Why exactly would he do that?"

"Because he doesn't think you two did all you could to help or stop his brother. I agree."

Of course, Kirk and Leeroy would believe that, but judging from Egan's disgusted expression, he wasn't buying this. After all, Kirk had thought Leeroy was there to find Tori. It was possible that Leeroy had concocted the story about a possible lawsuit to cover for the fact that he was indeed looking for Tori.

"Are you sure you didn't go to Kirk's house to plant a gun?" Egan snapped. "A gun that maybe you used to kill a woman?"

"No way in hell," Leeroy practically shouted. "Is that what the weasel Kirk said I did?"

Apparently, Leeroy wasn't feeling so good now about his possible alliance with the brother of his daughter's killer.

"I'm saying it," Egan clarified, and he sounded very much like the formidable sheriff that he was. "The timing of your visit is suspicious. You show up at Kirk's house and only an hour later, my deputies find a gun there."

"A gun they must have planted." Leeroy

grumbled something else she didn't catch. "Was it really used to kill that woman?"

"I don't know. It's at the lab now for testing. Is there a chance your prints or DNA will be on it?" Egan demanded.

"None. Well, unless someone stole a gun from my place and planted it at Kirk's. What kind of gun was it?"

"What kind of guns do you own?" Egan fired back. "And remember, I can check to see if you're lying."

"There's no reason for me to lie about that. I own a couple of hunting rifles, a shotgun and two handguns. One is a Glock 43, and the other is a .38 Smith & Wesson."

Bingo. The gun found at Kirk's was a .38 Smith & Wesson, and the dead woman had been killed with a .38. But why would Leeroy have killed her? The woman wasn't even one of Shanna's organ recipients.

Maybe it had been a case of mistaken identity. If Leeroy had been targeting Tori, he could have accidentally kidnapped Lorena by mistake. But if he had planned something like that, why would he have used his own gun? Maybe he'd simply messed up and then tried to cover his tracks by planting the gun at Kirk's.

"How much longer am I going to have to wait around here for you to show up?" Leeroy snarled.

"Maybe a long time. I'm not sure when I'll be in my office." Egan had probably told Leeroy that since he didn't want him to know that they would be traveling there soon. If Leeroy was behind the attacks, then it was best not to let him know their plans so he could send that sniper after them again.

"You expect me to just keep waiting for you?" Leeroy howled. "I've wasted enough time with your witch-hunt accusations."

"Yes, you're going to wait. My advice? Call a lawyer because you're going to need one if that gun in question turns out to be yours."

Egan didn't give Leeroy a chance to argue with that—something the man would have almost certainly done. Egan just ended the call.

"You think Leeroy will try to leave?" she asked.

"I hope so because then Thea can arrest him. That'll get him off the streets while we try to work out if he's behind the attacks."

True. But just because Leeroy was behind

bars, it wouldn't mean the sniper couldn't come after them again. If Leeroy had hired the gunmen, then he could hire others even if he happened to be in jail.

"Ian's ready," Egan told her, and he looked at her as if he wanted to say more. Maybe remind her to be careful when she went outside. If so, it was unnecessary. Jordan knew they were still in danger.

They started toward the front door when Egan's phone rang, and she saw Court's name on the screen. Egan answered it right away, and as he'd done with his other calls, he put it on speaker.

"Please tell me the gunman didn't go after you," Egan immediately said to his brother.

"No. But it looks as if he went after someone." Court paused, then cursed. "We have another dead body."

Chapter Eleven

Egan still had enough adrenaline left over from the attack, but hearing his brother's words gave him a jolt of even more. Jordan must have felt the same thing because the color drained from her face, and she dropped down into the chair next to her.

"Who was killed?" Egan asked Court.

"I can't tell yet. But it's a woman, and she was obviously murdered. It's pretty…messy."

So, there'd been blood and lots of it.

"The victim is a woman, and it appears she was killed at point-blank range with gunshot wounds to the head—just like our other victim. The body was on the road not far before the turn into town," Court added.

That was fairly close to where Lorena's body had been dumped. That meant the escaped sniper could have tossed her out there after he'd fled from the ranch. Or maybe there was a third hired thug who'd done the job.

One thing was certain, Egan knew that Leeroy or Kirk hadn't personally dumped the body because they'd been at the sheriff's office not only during the attack but in the time following it. If either of them had left the building, Thea would have told him about it.

That left Christian. The cop certainly hadn't been under Thea's watchful eye so he could have been the actual sniper. As a cop, he certainly would have had the firearm skill to pull off an attack like that.

"Could the body be Irene Adair?" Jordan's voice was so hoarse that Egan had to repeat the question to Court.

"Possibly. She's the woman who got one of Shanna's organs, right?"

"Yeah," Egan verified. "I don't have a picture of her, but her file is on my work computer. There's contact info in there for her and her family."

"I'll check," Court assured him. "I'm waiting with the body until the medical examiner, CSIs and a reserve deputy arrive. They were on their way out to you, but I think they need to process this scene first since it's closed down the road."

Egan agreed. It wasn't pleasant having a dead guy on the ranch, but the body on the road might give them more clues about the attacks than a hired gun would. Of course, he wanted answers from both bodies and both scenes. Maybe, just maybe, he'd get them, too.

"Is Dad with you?" Egan asked.

"No. The hands are dropping him off now at Griff's. They'll head back here to wait with me once they're done with that."

Good. Even though Court didn't seem to be the target of this sick piece of work who was behind these attacks, Egan didn't want his brother out there alone where he could be an easy target. Besides, their attacker could use Court to try to get to Jordan and him.

"I'm thinking it's not a good idea for you to have Jordan out on the road right now," Court added.

Egan was thinking the same thing. The body could have been left there as a way to draw them out into the open. As the sheriff, he wanted to see the crime scene firsthand, but that would be way too risky. Of course, there wasn't exactly a safe place for him to take Jordan to make sure the sniper didn't get to her again.

"You can use my place," Court said, no doubt knowing what was on Egan's mind. "Or the guesthouse or the fishing cabin."

Court's house and the cabin were at the back of the property. The guesthouse was much closer, which would cut down on the risk of Jordan being outside any longer than necessary. Still, there was a problem. Jordan and he had been lovers there, and he was sure every room would bring back memories. One look at Jordan, and he knew she'd be remembering the same thing. That was better, though, than having her stay in the main house with the shot-up windows.

"The guesthouse," Egan finally answered. "Once we're there, I'll have some of the hands help guard the place so I can send Ian back to work."

"You can keep him there if you want," Court suggested.

It was tempting, but the sheriff's office was already short of help because of the first murder investigation and the attacks. Now, with a second murder, a dead gunman and missing sniper, Court would need all the help he could get. No way could Egan justify tying up a deputy—even if that was what he wanted to do.

Twice now someone had come close to killing Jordan. Too close. And even though the hands were good with weapons, they weren't cops. Plus, the ranch was a big place, and it would be fairly easy for someone to sneak in on foot. The dead gunman outside the house was proof of that. Despite all of that, Egan was running out of options, and the guesthouse was the safest solution right now.

"Is it okay if I call Thea right now and have her reschedule Kirk's and Leeroy's interviews?" Court asked.

"Yes, do that." With everything going on, it was possible that Thea could end up manning the office alone, and Egan didn't want her there by herself with not one but two of their suspects. "Also have Thea remind Tori that she could be in danger and that she needs to be careful when she leaves."

"I will. And I'll call you once the medical examiner and reserve deputy are here to take over the crime scene," Court added. "It's possible the dead woman has an ID on her. She has a wallet sticking out of her pocket, but I don't want to touch it until the CSIs have had a look at it."

"If it's Irene, she'll have a scar on her belly from the transplant surgery," Jordan said, getting to her feet.

"I can't see her stomach. She's wearing jeans, but she has a lot of stab wounds on her torso."

Again, like their other victim. It ate away at him that this monster was doing this to innocent women. It was obviously having the same effect on Jordan because she shuddered and closed her eyes for a moment.

Even though Egan knew he should keep his hands off her, it was hard to do with that fear in her eyes. Not just fear for herself, either, but because this snake might include him and others in the killings. Egan slipped his arm around her, pulled her to him and brushed a kiss on the top of her head. It wasn't nearly as intimate as the other kiss had been, but it still reminded him that every time he got close to her like this, he was playing with fire.

And losing focus.

The first one might land them in bed, but the second one could get them killed, and that was why he eased back from her.

"We should go to the guesthouse," he said. He grabbed his laptop and the bag of supplies he'd gathered, and he got Jordan moving toward the door.

There were signs of the attack all around them. His father's blood in the doorway. The bits and pieces of wood that the bullets had torn from the door frame. There was broken glass on the porch. Of course, the worst sign was the dead gunman, and Jordan gave the guy more than a lingering glance when Egan was getting her into the back seat of the cruiser.

"You did what you had to do," Egan assured her.

He knew the assurance wouldn't mean much, but he had no idea what else to say. He'd killed someone once in the line of duty, and it wasn't something you forget. Jordan would carry this with her for the rest of her life, and she was already carrying too much baggage from Shanna's death. Now she was probably blaming herself for the two dead women, too. Egan got confirmation of that when he saw the tears shimmering in her eyes.

It was blurring more of those boundaries between them, but Egan still slipped his arm around her. As she'd done in the house, Jordan settled against him, reminding him of just how stupid that kiss had been. Because everything no longer felt like old times between them. It felt just as it had years ago when they'd first felt the attraction for each other.

Yeah, definitely a distraction.

Thankfully, it was a very short drive to the guesthouse. In fact, they could have easily walked if this had been a normal situation. It wasn't. But Egan used the couple of minutes to fill Ian in on the plan for him to return to the sheriff's office. Egan also texted Art, their ranch hand, to let him know that there would need to be someone watching not only the guesthouse but also the road that led to the ranch. Egan didn't want any surprise visitors, though if the sniper returned, he likely wouldn't use the road but would rather sneak onto the grounds.

When Ian pulled to a stop directly in front of the guesthouse, Egan got out first so he could unlock the front door and have a look around. It didn't take long since it was basically a living room-kitchen combo area, a bedroom and bathroom. Once he was certain that no one was lurking inside, he went back to the cruiser to hurry Jordan inside. He didn't waste any time locking the door and setting the security system.

"The windows are wired, too," he let her know. He hoped that would cause some of the tension to leave her face. It didn't, though.

Jordan stood in the living room and glanced around before her attention came back to him. She didn't say anything, but he figured she had noticed that the place hadn't changed that much since they'd last been here. His mom had had it redecorated a little with some fresh paint and a new sofa, but that was it. Once she went into the bedroom, she would see that it was the same, too.

"There should be bottled water in the fridge if you're thirsty," Egan explained. "There's also soup and stuff in the pantry, but I can have someone bring us in something to eat. There's plenty of food in the main house."

"Thanks. Maybe later I'll be hungry."

Egan wasn't counting on that. Her stomach was probably turning the same way his was. Still, she would have to eat something soon.

He went to the window to check and see if Ian had already driven away. He had. But

Egan also saw two hands drive up in a truck. Maybe they wouldn't have to stand guard for long, but he wanted them there at least until the deputies showed up with the medical examiner and the CSIs. Considering they were just now getting to the other body, though, that might be at least several hours.

"Maybe you should try to get some rest," Egan added.

She nodded, scrubbed her hands along the sides of her jeans. In addition to the fatigue and weariness, Jordan's nerves were showing. Maybe because of the leftover adrenaline from the attack. Or maybe just because of him. Egan was certainly feeling some nerves, too.

Jordan started for the sofa, but before she even made it there, her phone rang. She huffed when she looked at the screen and then showed him the name of the caller.

Christian.

"I can talk to him if you like," Egan offered.

"Thanks, but I can do it." She pressed the answer button, put it on speaker and then laid her phone on the coffee table as she sank down onto the sofa.

"Jordan, are you okay?" Christian immediately asked. "I just heard about the attack at the ranch."

"Who told you?" Jordan fired back.

He didn't jump to answer that, maybe because Jordan's tone had been so sharp. "A fellow cop. He has a friend in the medical examiner's office. Did you really have to kill a gunman?"

"Yes. What did your cop friend tell you about that?" Again, her tone wasn't exactly friendly.

That was probably why Christian muttered some profanity. "I can tell that Egan's turned you against me."

Blowing out a heavy breath, Jordan groaned and leaned the back of her head against the sofa. "Was there a reason you're calling? Because I'm tired, and I don't want to have another argument with you."

"Yes, there's a reason," Christian practically growled. "The criminal informant who told me about Kirk being at the chop shop is missing. He was supposed to meet me so I could pay him for some information he'd given me, but he didn't show. That's definitely not like him. When money's involved, he doesn't miss our meetings."

"You think someone silenced him?" Egan asked.

Judging from the huff Christian made, he hadn't known the call was on speaker and that Egan was listening. "Yes, that's exactly what I think, and this is on your shoulders. You should have found and arrested the person responsible for these attacks. If you'd done your job, Jordan wouldn't be in danger and my CI wouldn't be missing."

Egan agreed, but he hadn't failed at finding the person from lack of trying. And he would continue to try. "Let me know if your CI turns up," Egan insisted.

Since that definitely sounded like a goodbye, Egan expected Christian to end the call. He didn't.

"I think someone's been following me," Christian said after a short pause. "I just want to make sure it's not one of your deputies."

"It's not." Now it was Egan's turn to pause. He wasn't sure that Christian was telling the truth, but if he was innocent, then it was entirely possible that the killer had the cop in his sights.

"Then I'll have to watch my back," Christian grumbled, and he ended the call.

Jordan immediately looked up at Egan. "Christian could have said that to make himself seem innocent."

Egan nodded. "And that's why I want to keep digging in the cold cases you've been researching." He brought his laptop to her. "If you could access the file, I can work on that while you get some rest."

Jordan shook her head but then winced a little when her shoulder moved, as well. She was no doubt still in pain from the fresh stitches. "We can work on them together."

Since Egan knew the pain would only get worse, he went to the medicine cabinet in the bathroom and came back with some over-the-counter stuff. "It won't make you drowsy," he reminded her, and he gave her a bottle of water so she could take two of the pills.

"Thanks." She didn't look at him when he sat next to her. And Egan knew why. Even with the interference from the pain, the left-over heat from that kiss was still zinging between them, and it was best not to tempt fate by kissing again.

She opened the files and went to the two

cases that she had already pointed out to him when they'd been at the sheriff's office. Egan moved the computer to his lap so he could have a closer look. Not at the files themselves. But rather at Jordan's notes.

"You've been suspicious of Christian for a couple of weeks now," he pointed out.

"Yes. I keep going back to the theory that he could have been, or still could be, running a human trafficking ring." She paused. "Since Shanna was the parole officer for both men associated with this case, I wonder if one of them mentioned something to her about that."

"You mean something that would have incriminated Christian as their boss," Egan finished for her.

She nodded, and now she looked at him. But it wasn't heat and attraction he saw in her eyes now. It was a boatload of concern. "If so, Christian could have wanted to silence her by setting up Drew Paxton to murder her."

Egan had already reached that same conclusion, but it still felt like a punch to the gut to hear it spelled out for him. Drew had been the one to pull the trigger and put a bullet in Shanna, but if Christian had provoked him in some way to do that, then Christian was equally guilty of her murder.

But that was a big *if*.

Leeroy and Kirk might not have had anything to do with Shanna's murder, but either of them could be behind these attacks. What they needed was an ID on the gunman Jordan had killed, and they might be able to link him to one of the suspects. Right now, that seemed their best shot at solving this.

Egan took out his phone to see if there was a CSI available to come to the ranch, but his phone dinged before he could make the call, and it was Court's name that popped up on the screen.

"Is everything okay?" Egan asked the moment he answered.

"More or less. I'm still at the crime scene with the dead woman. The CSIs just arrived, and I had them check the wallet first. No driver's license, but there's a photo ID. It's Irene Adair."

Jordan's arm was right against his so he felt her go stiff. Of course, they'd been expecting this, but there was no way to prepare for hearing that another of Shanna's recipients had been murdered.

"Of course, I'll get her next of kin to confirm it, but the woman matches her photo, and it's a legit ID from where she works."

Egan didn't doubt this was indeed Irene. But he still didn't know if her murder was actually connected to Shanna or if someone just wanted to make it look that way.

"Any chance you can spare one of the CSIs?" Egan asked. "I'd like them to take a look at the dead guy here at the ranch."

"There are three here, and I'll send out one of them. I'll see if Griff can spare someone from the rangers, too."

Egan thanked him, ended the call and then turned to Jordan to see how she was handling this. Not well. Her eyes had watered, the tears threatening, and her bottom lip was trembling.

"This has to end," she whispered. Jordan was still fighting the tears, but it was a battle she was losing.

Egan wasn't immune to those tears, either. Seeing her like this caused his chest to tighten until it felt as if someone had latched on to his heart and was squeezing hard. He had no idea what to do to make this better. But he apparently had a bad way of trying to fix it.

He kissed her.

He felt her go stiff, probably because she was stunned that he was doing this. Egan was stunned, too. Kissing Jordan was the last thing that should be on his mind, but he didn't stop. In fact, he made things worse by pulling her to him. She not only landed in his arms. Jordan also slid her hands around the back of his neck.

She made a sound of pleasure. Something soft and silky. Something that loosened up the muscles in his chest, but it tightened other parts of him. Specifically, that stupid part of him behind the zipper of his jeans. The kiss was reminding him of the times when they'd been lovers, and it was starting to feel more like foreplay than just a simple kiss. Of course, nothing stayed simple when it came to Jordan and him.

Egan was mindful of her injury and tried not to hurt her, but he deepened the kiss. And the taste of her slammed through him. It was a familiar taste, one that stirred not just the old memories but also the heat and the attraction that was quickly racing out of control.

That still didn't stop him.

He kept kissing her. And Jordan certainly wasn't doing anything to stop it or even slow it down. She lowered her hand from his neck, sliding her palm down his back until she reached the waist of his jeans. This was the problem with them being past lovers. It was the next step of foreplay for her to go after his zipper. And for him to go after hers. But Egan couldn't risk having sex with her now. Even if that was exactly what his body wanted him to do.

He pulled back from her at the exact moment that she pulled away from him. For a moment he thought that was a timely coincidence, but then he felt her take out her phone from her pocket.

"I had it set on vibrate," she said. "And I have a call."

Egan was actually thankful for the interruption. At least he was thankful until he saw the screen.

Unknown Caller.

Hell, this couldn't be good.

Jordan looked at him, silently asking him what to do. "Answer it," he said. "But put it on speaker."

She gave a shaky nod and did as he said. It didn't take long for the caller to start talking. "Jordan," he growled.

At least Egan thought the caller was male. It was hard to tell because he seemed to be speaking through some sort of voice scrambler.

"Who is this?" Egan demanded.

Again, it didn't take long for the guy to respond. "I'm the person who'll kill Jordan, and there's nothing you can do to stop me."

Chapter Twelve

I'm the person who'll kill Jordan.

Jordan had no trouble hearing what the caller had just said. No trouble believing that was his intention, either. And it sent a chill straight through her. Egan had a different reaction, though. He cursed and snatched the phone from her.

"Who the hell is this?" Egan snapped.

"Oh, you want my name? Sorry, but you can't have that." And it sounded as if the caller laughed. "If you want to catch me, you'll have to do your job. I'm not going to make this easy for you."

This could be someone playing a hoax, but she didn't think so. No. This was the real deal. The man behind the attacks and murders along with being the person who'd left that note with Lorena Lovett.

"What do you want?" Jordan asked. She was glad that her voice sounded a lot stronger than she felt.

"First of all, don't bother to trace this call. It's a burner cell. No way to find me with a trace. And now that we've got that out of the way, here's what I want you to do. Meet with me. Just you and me. You can't bring Egan with you. Then you and I will have a little chat."

"You mean a chat where you'll try to kill me," Jordan said.

The caller certainly didn't jump to deny that. "You have to admit you've been living on borrowed time. Drew Paxton's bullet hit you in the side and damaged both your kidneys so badly that you needed a transplant. If it weren't for Shanna, you'd be dead by now."

That sounded like something Leeroy would say. Of course, the person could want them to think that Shanna's father was responsible.

"You want to put an end to the attacks and the killings?" the caller went on. "You want to save Egan?"

"You know I do." She didn't even have to think about that.

"But saving me isn't what you have in

mind," Egan said to the caller. "You want to use me to get to Jordan. I have something different in mind. I want you to stop these games and turn yourself in to the cops."

He laughed again. "Dream on, cowboy. That's not going to happen. But you and I can put an end to things if you'll just have that chat with me. I'll tell you all about why I've done these things."

"Dream on," Egan repeated like venom. "Because Jordan's not meeting with you."

"Too bad because that means someone else will die."

There was another sound. Not laughter this time, but Jordan couldn't tell what it was since it was filtered through the scrambler. However, it sounded as if someone was with the caller.

Oh, mercy.

The fear slid through her again, and she prayed this snake didn't have another soon-to-be victim with him.

"Haven't you killed enough?" Jordan pleaded with him. "Please, just let this end."

"I've told you the only way it can end. By meeting with me. But I can tell that's not going to happen. That's okay. But just remember—you could have stopped this, and you didn't."

Even though the scrambler was still on, Jordan was certain of the next sound.

A scream.

The kind of scream a person made when they were in severe pain. Terrified. Or being murdered.

"Stop, please!" Jordan shouted into the phone.

But she was talking to the air because the caller had already hung up.

Jordan immediately turned to Egan, hoping that he could stop whatever was happening. She knew that wasn't possible, though. They didn't even know where the caller was.

"The scream could have been fake," he reminded her, and he took out his own phone.

Jordan so wanted to latch on to that and believe it. And it very well could be true. The caller obviously wanted to draw her out into the open so he could kill her, and an easy way to do that was to make her think someone was being hurt, or worse, because of her.

"Text Thea and give her the caller's number," Egan instructed. "It's a long shot, but he might have lied about it being a burner."

True, and while Jordan sent that text, Egan made a call. Not to Court or one of the other deputies. Instead, he pressed Leeroy's number, and the man answered on the first ring.

"What do you want now, Egan?" Leeroy barked.

"Where are you?" Egan snapped right back.

"I'm about to head home. If you're calling to have me come back in for questioning, don't bother. Thea already set me up with another appointment for tomorrow morning."

If Leeroy had been the one to make that scrambled call, he certainly wasn't showing any signs of it. He sounded as angry and ornery as he usually was. Of course, that could be an act. He could have put away the burner cell and scrambler to answer the call from Egan.

"Don't be late for your interview tomorrow," Egan warned the man.

He ended the call and immediately went to one of their other suspects. Christian. Unlike Leeroy, however, he didn't answer.

"I can call Christian's office at San Antonio PD," Jordan offered.

She waited for Egan to nod in agreement before she searched through her contacts and found the number for Detective Marvin Daniels, Christian's partner. And he did answer almost right away.

"This is Jordan Gentry," she greeted. "I'm trying to get in touch with Christian—"

"So am I," Marvin interrupted. "What the hell is going on with him?"

That certainly wasn't the response she'd expected. "What do you mean?"

"He just called me and said someone tried to kill him."

Jordan tamped down the slam of emotions and tried to see both sides of this. Yes, someone could have attacked Christian, but it was possible this was part of the ruse to make him look innocent.

"How long ago did Christian call you?" Jordan asked.

"Five minutes or so. Maybe a little longer. Why?"

If it was longer, then that would have been when Egan was still on the phone with the scrambled caller. And that meant it couldn't have been Christian. Of course, that didn't mean he couldn't have hired someone to make that call.

"Jordan?" Marvin pressed when she didn't say anything.

"I'm not sure what's going on," she answered. "Do you have any idea if Christian is all right?"

"I don't know. I'm on the way to the hospital now."

"Hospital?" Jordan repeated on a rise of breath. If this was a ruse, then Christian was making it look very real.

"Yeah. He's driving himself there, so I don't know how bad he's hurt. You want me to have him get in touch with you when he can?"

"No. That's all right. But if you could text me and let me know his condition, I'd appreciate it."

"Will do," Marvin agreed before he hung up.

She looked at Egan again to see his reaction to what they'd just heard about Christian, but he had already moved on to calling their third and final suspect, Kirk. While Egan was waiting for him to answer, however, he got another call from Thea, and he immediately answered it.

"I'm pretty sure I know the answer to this, but I have to ask. By any chance did you leave your truck on Smith Road by the Welcome to McCall Canyon sign?" Thea asked.

"No. It's still in the repair shop."

"That's what I figured. Well, there's a truck identical to yours back there. I'm thinking it's the one used in the attack since the windshield is shot up. And guess who found it?"

"Kirk?"

"Leeroy," Thea answered. "He says he spotted it a couple of minutes ago when he was driving home."

That was possible since Smith Road led to his place. Still, it seemed a huge coincidence that one of their suspects would be the one to find it. Unless someone had set it up so that Leeroy would be the one who stumbled on it. Plus, it sounded as if the truck hadn't exactly been hidden away.

"Please tell me that Leeroy didn't touch the vehicle," Egan said.

"He claims he didn't. Griff and I are on our way there now to check it out, and I told Leeroy to get back in his own truck and wait for us," Thea went on. "He said he would, but he claims that there's blood on the outside of the door."

"The killer threw the dead woman out of

the truck," Egan reminded her. "And she'd been shot and stabbed so it could have gotten there then."

"Yeah," Thea agreed. Then, she paused. "But Leeroy is insisting this blood isn't from the other attack. He's saying this is *fresh*."

FRESH BLOOD.

That was *not* what Egan wanted to hear. Especially coming on the heels of the phone call from a thug claiming that he would kill someone else if Jordan didn't meet with him. This might not even be connected to that call, but Jordan would almost certainly think it was.

"Call me when you get to the truck," Egan insisted. "And if the connection's good enough, make it a video call so I can see what's going on."

"Will do," Thea assured him before she hung up.

Even though it would likely be only a few minutes before Thea and Griff got there, he wanted to use that short amount of time to try to calm that look on Jordan's face. And this time, he wouldn't kiss her to do that.

"Leeroy could be wrong. It might not be fresh blood," he reminded her. "And even if it is, he might have been the one who planted it there."

She nodded, but the agreement didn't quite make it to her eyes. "I need to figure out a way to stop this."

Since she looked ready to panic—or agree to the meeting that the killer wanted—Egan took her by the shoulders. "Someone could have set all of this up just to draw you out."

"But Irene—"

"She could have been dead long before the thug called you and asked you to meet him."

Jordan still didn't look convinced so Egan pulled her into his arms. No kiss. But he did hold her. It wasn't much, but then there wasn't a lot he could do to help her until he caught the piece of dirt who was behind all of this.

His phone rang, and Egan answered it right away when he saw Thea's name on the screen.

"We're pulling up to the truck now," Thea said the moment she was on the line. Just as they'd agreed, it was a video call with audio so he could see Thea. "Leeroy's sitting in his own vehicle just like I told him to do."

Good. That was something at least. If they found any prints or DNA from Leeroy, Egan didn't want the man claiming that it had gotten there just now because he'd touched something.

"Leeroy's getting out of his truck," Thea went on, "but I'll have Griff deal with him while I take a closer look."

Thea turned the phone in the direction of the truck as she approached it, and Jordan stood right next to him, watching and listening to everything. The truck was indeed identical to his, including the license plates, which were obviously a fake duplicate. It wouldn't have been especially hard for someone to create a bogus tag, but it did let Egan know that this person had gone to a lot of trouble to make everyone believe that he'd been the one behind the murder.

But why?

Egan could only guess about that, but it might have been so that he would be blamed for Lorena's, and Jordan's, murders. For that to happen, though, there would have had to be a witness. There hadn't been. But since the attack had happened on a road, maybe the killer had been planning for any contingency.

Thea continued to move closer to the truck, and in the background Egan could hear Leeroy arguing with Griff. He didn't catch every word that Leeroy was saying, but the gist was that Leeroy was worried about being blamed for this. Of course, that could be all hot air since maybe he was indeed responsible.

"There's the blood," Thea said, aiming her phone camera at the driver's-side door. There was certainly something there. And it looked like blood spatter. The kind of spatter that could result from a gunshot wound or high-velocity spatter from an impact wound.

"I don't want to touch the door handle," Thea said. "There might be prints or DNA on it."

Egan was about to agree with her, but then he heard Thea mumble some profanity. "There's a body on the floor by the passenger's seat."

Jordan gasped and touched her fingers to her mouth. She hadn't exactly looked steady before Thea's second call, but now it was worse.

"Is it Tori?" Jordan asked.

"No. It's a man. And I think he's alive. Griff, call an ambulance," Thea shouted, and while she was still holding her phone, she hurried to the passenger's door and threw it open. There was indeed a man on the floor, and he was in between the seat and the dash. His hands were tied, and he had a gag around his mouth. But Egan had no trouble recognizing him.

It was Kirk.

And he was alive. He was moaning.

"Kirk," Jordan muttered under her breath. She didn't say more, but Egan figured she was thinking the same thing he was—that Kirk was no longer a suspect. Well, maybe he was. Kirk could have set this up.

Or not.

"He's been shot," Thea said. And that had Egan rethinking his theory that Kirk could have done this to himself. It seemed an extreme way to make them believe he was innocent.

Thea set her phone down on the seat, and while it wasn't a perfect angle, Egan could still see the man. There was blood on Kirk's shoulder and chest, but the moment Thea untied the gag from his mouth, he opened his eyes. His face was tight, his forehead bunched up, and he was still moaning in pain.

"The ambulance will be here in a few minutes," Griff called out.

Good. Because Egan didn't want Kirk dying

before he had a chance to answer a whole lot of questions. Egan went ahead with the first question on his list.

"Who did this to you?" Egan asked.

Kirk moaned again and shook his head. "A big guy. He was hiding in the back seat of my car, and I didn't see him until it was too late." Kirk glanced around. "Where am I? How did I get here?"

Egan wanted to curse. Either Kirk had been unconscious after he was shot or else he was going to claim that he was. Too bad because that meant the man couldn't give them critical details.

"Was Tori with you when you were shot?" Jordan asked.

"No. She left in her own car." Kirk shook his head, and his eyelids fluttered down, threatening to close. If the man was faking this, he was doing a good job because he definitely looked in pain and as if he were fighting to remain conscious.

"Did the shooter say anything to you before he shot you?" Egan pressed.

"No." Kirk didn't hesitate with that answer, but he did pause right afterward. "I think he was just a hired gun."

Probably, but it didn't explain why the guy would have moved Kirk from his car to the truck. Obviously, the person behind this had wanted the truck to be found, but did that mean the plan had been to leave Kirk alive? Egan just didn't know, and he might not have the answer to that until Kirk got to the hospital. If his injury was life-threatening, then maybe the hired gun had figured he would just bleed out.

But why hadn't he just made sure that Kirk was dead?

"I think I know who set the thug on me," Kirk said. His voice was even weaker now. "I think it was Tori."

Of all the things that Egan had thought Kirk might say, that wasn't one of them. "Tori?" Egan and Jordan questioned at the same time. It was Egan who continued, "Why would she have hired someone to kill you?"

Kirk mumbled something that Egan didn't catch and then he winced in pain. "Because Tori found out that I knew about her."

Egan would have definitely pressed for more info about that, but Kirk's head dropped to the side, landing against the dash, and his eyes closed. Thea immediately pressed her fingers to the man's neck.

"He's still alive, but he needs to get to the hospital," Thea said, urgency in her voice. In the background, Egan could hear a welcome sound. The sirens from the ambulance.

"Go with him in the ambulance," Egan instructed Thea. "If he regains consciousness, ask him about Tori."

"I will, but Kirk's lost a lot of blood. You think maybe he was just talking out of his head?"

Egan didn't know, but he would do everything to find out. "Just let me know whatever Kirk says," Egan instructed.

He ended the call, turning to Jordan to see if she had any idea about this, but she shook her head. *"Because Tori found out that I knew about her,"* she repeated. "What would Kirk have learned?"

But she didn't wait for him to answer. Jordan went to the laptop and accessed the files from her storage cloud. "I had info on the transplant recipients, but I don't think anything is in here that would give us a clue."

Neither did he. Because if there had been something, Jordan would have already connected the dots. Still, she scanned through the details she'd saved. However, Egan's thoughts went in a different direction.

"We both thought it was strange that Tori would be Kirk's lawyer," Egan said, thinking out loud. "But what if Tori also knew Drew?"

Jordan immediately looked at him. "I didn't even look for a connection like that."

There would have been no reason for her to do that. She'd been researching the organ recipients to find out who might want all of them dead, but Drew didn't seem to be a viable suspect since he'd had no way to arrange for hired guns. Because he was on death row, all of his visits and correspondence were carefully monitored.

Jordan exited the storage files and instead did an internet search on Tori. "There's not a lot," she said. "She's only been a lawyer..." She stopped. "When she was still in law school, she interned at the law firm that defended Drew."

That caused a bad feeling to snake up his spine. "You have the number for that firm?" he asked, taking out his phone again.

Egan pressed in the number as Jordan rattled it off, and it took him several minutes to work his way through to someone who might know anything about Tori. He was eventually connected to the head of personnel for the law firm, Stanley Clark. He put the call on speaker so that Jordan would be able to hear it.

"I'm Sheriff Egan McCall," he greeted the man, "and I need info on one of your former interns, Tori Judd. It's important. She could be in danger." Egan wouldn't mention that she might have had part in shooting in a man.

"Danger," Stanley repeated. "Does this have anything to do with her heart transplant?"

So, the man knew her. That was a good start. "Maybe indirectly."

"That's a shame. She was really sick when she worked here, and I'd hoped the heart transplant would give her a chance at life. Did her body reject the heart or something?"

"I'm not sure." Yeah, it was a lie, but this guy might clam up if he realized this was a murder investigation. "By any chance, did Tori work on the Drew Paxton murder trial?"

Silence. For a long time. And that silence was a red flag for Egan. "It's important," Egan repeated. "I believe she's been getting threats."

"No. She didn't work on his murder trial, but she did on his previous narcotics conviction."

That was the conviction that had put Drew on parole with Shanna as his parole officer. "Tori worked directly with Drew on the trial?" Egan pressed.

Stanley sighed. "Yes. Everybody warned Tori to keep her distance from that man, but she didn't listen. Maybe because that was about the time she was getting so sick."

Or maybe Tori had a thing for bad boys. And Drew was the ultimate bad boy.

"Anyway," Stanley went on, "I don't believe anything inappropriate went on between them, but a lot of people thought Tori had allowed herself to get too close to him. It didn't matter, though, because after the transplant, she went to work for another law firm." Stanley paused. "Is Drew Paxton the one who's threatening her?"

"Possibly. Do you know anything about that?"

"Nothing concrete, but I got the feeling that he'd developed a fixation on her, and I thought the man was bad news. I was right because I've heard he's in jail again for murder."

"He is." And Egan hated that just talking about the snake brought all the bad memories back to the surface. "Do you have any idea if Tori stayed in touch with Drew after his drug conviction?"

"There were rumors that she saw him, but like I said, she went to work for another firm, and I lost contact with her after that."

Too bad that had happened because Egan needed to know just how close Tori had gotten to Drew and if it was connected to everything that was going on right now.

"If you remember anything else about Tori, please let me know," Egan told Stanley.

Egan ended the call and immediately pressed in Tori's number again. No answer. However, he did leave her a message to contact him ASAP. When his phone buzzed with an incoming message, Egan thought maybe she was calling him, but it was Court.

"Griff just filled me in on what happened with Kirk," Court said when Egan answered. "You want me to go to the hospital?"

It was tempting because Court was good at interrogation, but Egan needed him to man the office and work the murder investigation.

And if Kirk didn't make it, they'd have another murder to try to solve.

"No. Stay put," Egan answered. "I just found out that Tori knew Drew, so Jordan and I will be working on that."

"She what?" Court added some ripe curse words to go with that.

Surprise had been Egan's reaction, too, and it wasn't a good thing that Tori hadn't volunteered that info. A connection to Drew meant she could also be connected to the attacks and killings, and that was probably the reason she hadn't volunteered that to him.

"If you need any help with the Tori angle, let me know," Court went on. "In the meantime, the reason I called was to let you know that a pair of CSIs are on the ranch, and they're examining the dead guy. No ID on him, but they'll take his prints and run those ASAP."

"Thanks." The sooner they knew who the guy was, the sooner they could use him to try to link him to one of their suspects. Of course, their suspect list was changing. Egan was adding Tori as a person of interest, and Kirk had dropped to the bottom. If Kirk had merely wanted to give himself an injury so that he looked innocent, he wouldn't have taken things that far. Well, unless something had gone seriously wrong with whatever he'd planned.

When he finished his call with Court, he saw that Jordan was already doing a computer search on Tori. Good. Maybe she'd find something they could use.

Egan tried a different angle. He sent a text to the warden at the prison where Drew was incarcerated and asked if Tori had ever visited Drew or written him a letter. Even if there was no record of the letter, it didn't mean the two hadn't stayed in touch that way. Letters could often get past security by having a lawyer deliver them.

He debated calling Drew's lawyer, but the guy probably wasn't going to admit that he'd broken prison rules by bringing in letters from the outside. Still, it was worth a try. Anything was at this point. Well, anything other than Jordan surrendering herself to this killer.

Egan was about to use the computer to look up a number for Drew's attorney, but his phone rang again before he could do that. It wasn't Court this time. It was Thea, and he hoped she had good news.

"We just got to the hospital, and they took

Kirk into surgery," Thea said the moment Egan answered.

Well, at least he was still alive. "Any idea if he'll survive?"

"Not yet. The doctor didn't talk to me, but Kirk did. He woke up a couple of times while we were still in the ambulance."

That grabbed Egan's attention. Jordan's, too, because she stood and went closer to him. "What did he say?" Egan asked.

"I'm not sure it makes sense. Kirk was drifting in and out of consciousness so take this with a grain of salt. But Kirk mumbled that Drew found out something. Something important, he insisted. He said that Drew learned that Shanna was *the one*."

Jordan obviously heard that because she shook her head. "The one?" she repeated.

"A match," Thea clarified. "According to Kirk, Drew knew that Tori would be a match to get Shanna's heart. And that's why Drew killed Shanna."

Chapter Thirteen

Jordan heard every word Thea said, but it was hard for her to process it. For two years she'd believed the events of that fateful night had played out because of Drew's obsession with Shanna.

But had it all been a lie?

Judging from Egan's bunched-up forehead and stark expression, he was having trouble with it, too.

"Remember, Kirk might not have known what he was saying," Thea added. "Or he could have just made it up."

True, but what reasons would Kirk have had to lie about something like this? The only possibility that came to mind was that this lie was part of some semibotched attempt to make them believe he wasn't responsible for all the murders and attempted murders.

"Griff took Leeroy to the sheriff's office to get his statement about finding the truck," Thea went on. "But once he's done with that, he can go to the prison to talk to Drew. Or I could go," Thea continued when Egan didn't say anything. "I just don't think it's a good idea for you to try to talk to him right now." She paused. "Are you okay?"

Egan cleared his throat, and Jordan could see that he was trying to steel himself up. "Have Griff go out and talk to Drew," Egan finally answered. What he didn't do was address Thea's question if he was okay. He clearly wasn't.

Even if what Kirk had said was a lie, it was bringing back all the memories and grief for Egan. For Jordan, too. And this time the grief was worse. Something that she hadn't thought possible. But it was heartbreaking to think that Shanna might not have been killed by a madman after all. She might have been murdered because she could be an organ donor for Tori.

"I want you to stay at the hospital and keep watch," Egan added to Thea several moments later. "If someone did try to kill Kirk, they might come back and try to finish the job."

Oh, mercy.

With everything else going on, Jordan hadn't even considered that. But it was a possibility. And if the person succeeded in finishing off Kirk, that might prevent them from ever learning the truth. She seriously doubted they were going to get the truth from Drew.

Egan ended the call with Thea and then glanced around as if trying to figure out what to do. Finally, he groaned. Then cursed.

Jordan doubted he would want her to do this, but she slipped her arm around him anyway. He didn't push her away. Nor did he relax any. She still felt his rock-hard muscles.

Egan looked down at her, their eyes meeting, and Jordan got another jolt of that bone-deep pain they were both feeling. At least Egan didn't seem to be blaming her for that pain.

But she was still blaming herself.

Even if Drew had orchestrated the hostage situation with the ultimate goal of killing Shanna, Jordan should have still been able to stop him. If that was what Egan was feeling, though, he certainly didn't show it. In fact, he brushed a kiss on her mouth, causing her own muscles to tense. Then relax. He stared at her as if trying to decide if he wanted to kiss her again, but he obviously decided against that because he stepped away from her.

He scrubbed his hand over his face and groaned softly. "Focus," he grumbled under his breath, and when his attention came back to her again, he did seem all business. "How the hell would Drew have found out that Shanna was a donor, much less a match?" he asked.

She lifted her shoulder. "Maybe Drew saw it on her driver's license. Or hacked into the DMV database." Of course, it would have required him to do more than that. "He must have gotten into Shanna's medical records, too, for him to find out."

"But that would have only told him her blood type, right? Is there more to it than that?"

"There is. It's called cross-match typing, where they mix together blood from the donor and possible recipient. If the recipient's cells attack the donor cells, then the transplant will fail."

Egan huffed. "So, why would Drew have believed that Shanna was a match in the first place?"

Jordan had to think about that a few seconds. "Maybe because of Shanna's blood type. She was B-positive, which meant the recipients had to be either B or AB. I was AB," she added under her breath. "Only a small percentage of the population has that particular type."

And that meant she'd gotten very lucky to even have a donor. Of course, maybe Drew had created that "luck" by trying to get Tori a heart. He probably had no idea that Jordan would be a match for an organ transplant, too.

"If we can find Tori's blood type," she went on, "I'm betting it'll be B or AB." Well, it would if Kirk was telling the truth.

Egan made a sound of agreement. "Drew's target could have been Shanna all along. That's why he shot her in the head with a low-caliber gun." But he seemed to be talking more to himself than her. "He knew the shot probably wouldn't kill her immediately. That way, she'd linger on, and there'd be time to harvest her organs."

The relief came flooding through her. For a couple of seconds anyway. Maybe she hadn't been to blame for Shanna's death, but it certainly didn't feel like a victory. Because Shanna was still dead, and this was all just a theory. To prove it, they'd need a lot more information.

"I'll try to find out Tori's blood type," she offered. "I can use my phone to search for that if you need to use the laptop."

"I do. I want to read through the files that San Antonio PD collected on Drew for the murder trial. It's possible they included his internet searches."

Yes, and that way they could tell if Drew had been looking for ways to save Tori. And speaking of Tori, Egan tried one more time to call her, but it had the same results. No answer, and the call went to voice mail.

On another huff, Egan sank down on the sofa and got to work. So did Jordan, but she'd managed to search for only about five minutes when her phone rang. Jordan's heart nearly stopped when she saw *Unknown Caller* on the screen.

"This could be from the killer," she said to Egan.

He took out his own phone to record the call, and once he'd done that, he motioned for her to answer it. Jordan hit the answer button and pulled in her breath, waiting.

"It's me," the caller said. The voice wasn't

filtered through a scrambler this time, and it was someone she recognized.

Christian.

Jordan didn't especially want to have to deal with Christian now, but she did want to know if he'd indeed gone to the hospital. She took his call and put it on speaker for Egan.

"Why are you using an unknown number?" she asked.

"I thought it'd be smart to go with a burner cell in case someone's trying to track my location. You know, someone like you who wants to kill me. Why do you want me dead?" Christian snapped.

She hadn't thought anything he could say would surprise her, but that did it. "Why would you think that?"

"Because the thug who tried to kill me said you'd hired him."

The chill that ran through her was ice-cold. Not because there was any hint that it was true but because someone was trying to set her up. Well, maybe. Or Christian could be doing like Kirk might have and grasping at straws to make himself look innocent.

With a scowl on his face, Egan dropped

down next to her. "Who's the thug? And then tell me everything he said to you."

Christian cursed. "We didn't exchange names or introduce ourselves. The guy stepped out from the side of the building when I was going to my car. He said, 'This is for Jordan,' and he pulled the trigger."

Jordan nearly gasped. "He shot you?"

"Damn right, he did. He clipped me in the shoulder before I drew my gun. I shot at him, and he ran."

"And you didn't go after him?" There was a lot of skepticism in Egan's voice and question.

"No. Because I was bleeding and needed to get to the hospital. But now that I'm stitched up, I'll look for him."

That didn't make sense. "Why didn't you call someone from San Antonio PD to find him?" Jordan pressed. "The guy will be long gone by now."

"He'll be back. And that brings me to my original question. Why would you want me dead?"

"I don't, and I certainly didn't hire someone to kill you. Why would I?" she tossed right back at him.

"I've been giving that some thought, and I

think you might be trying to cover up something. Maybe something in one of those files you're reviewing for The Right Verdict. You couldn't just destroy the file because that would make them suspicious. So, maybe you're trying to set me up."

Jordan forced herself not to lash out, but that riled her. She hadn't been a dirty cop, and she wasn't dirty now. However, Christian could be.

"Your injury must not have been serious," she said, "if they didn't keep you in the hospital."

Christian cursed again. "I figured you'd tried to put all of this back on me. Just own up to whatever it is you're doing so this stops."

"I was about to ask you to do that same thing," Egan snarled. He ignored Christian's profanity-laced protest and kept on talking. "Someone just tried to kill Kirk Paxton, and he's not walking out of the ER with his injuries."

"Did Kirk say who hurt him?" Christian asked.

"Well, it wasn't some thug claiming that Jordan hired him. Not that we know of anyway. But whoever did it, it was probably the same person who called Jordan just minutes before that happened. He wanted Jordan to meet him so the killings would stop. You know anything about that?"

"No. I was too busy getting shot." Christian didn't rein in his sarcasm, but he did pause. "Did Kirk say anything?"

Egan's eyes narrowed with suspicion, and she knew why. That question sounded more than just a fishing expedition. Christian seemed concerned, or something.

"Kirk said a lot of things," Egan threw out there. "That's why I tried to call you earlier. I wanted to question you about some things he said."

Christian stayed quiet several moments. "If Kirk brought up my name, then he's a liar. Or else his attacker wanted to set me up…hell. I gotta go. I just spotted the guy who tried to kill me."

Jordan called out to Christian so that he wouldn't hang up. She wanted to tell him to call for backup. But he'd already ended the call.

Egan didn't waste any time calling San Antonio PD to let them know they might have an officer in danger. *Might.* Still, it was too big of a risk not to have someone at least try to help Christian.

Since she was feeling a little wobbly and her head was hurting, Jordan went back to the sofa. "Leeroy's the only one of our suspects who hasn't been hurt," she said. "And Tori."

Egan made such a quick sound of agreement that it meant it was something he'd already considered, and he sank down next to her to continue working on the laptop. "That doesn't mean either of them are innocent."

She nodded. "Leeroy or Tori could have intended to kill Christian, Kirk and me, and they could have simply failed." And that meant whoever was behind this would only keep coming back until the job was done.

Jordan didn't voice that last part aloud, but Egan must have picked up on it because he slid his arm around her and kissed her again. Like the other one, it was just a simple brush of his lips, and it landed on her forehead. She wasn't even certain he'd been aware he'd done it because his attention stayed on the computer screen.

"We'll have to wait for Drew's files to be emailed to me," he explained. "But the request is in. Any luck finding Tori's blood type?"

"No. Sorry." She lifted her phone to get back to doing that, but Egan took hold of her hand. At first, she didn't know why he had done that, but then Jordan realized she was trembling.

He frowned, maybe at the trembling. Maybe because he wasn't so pleased that he was touching her again. "You want to try to take that nap now?" he asked.

Jordan didn't even have to think how to answer that. "No. I wouldn't be able to sleep. Besides, I need to work on getting that information about Tori."

Egan stared at her, maybe trying to come up with some argument that would cause her to give in. But there was no good argument for that. Or at least that was what Jordan thought.

Until Egan kissed her again.

This time it wasn't some mindless peck on the forehead. It was a real kiss, and she immediately felt the heat and sensations that went along with it. Of course, she always felt that way whenever Egan got close. He was obviously doing this to comfort her, though, and she figured he would stop after only a few seconds.

He didn't.

The kiss continued, and he slipped his arm around her, pulling her closer to him. More heat came. More of that fire that'd been simmering between them since they were teenagers, but this particular fire was already flaming much too hot.

Jordan eased back, meeting his gaze. She expected to see some doubts there. But there were none. There was only a moment of silence before Egan pulled her back to him and kissed her again.

EGAN WAS ABOUT 90 percent certain that this was a mistake, but he held on to the remaining 10 percent as if it were a lifeline. Even if this was wrong and something he would almost certainly regret, it was what he needed.

And what Jordan needed, too.

She proved that when the sound of pleasure purred in her throat, and she kissed him right back. He hadn't needed anything to up the ante on this and make it feel like foreplay, but that did it.

He forced himself to think of the logistics of this. There was a CSI crew on the grounds, plenty of ranch hands, too, and any one of them might come to the door at any second.

If that happened, the foreplay would end, and Jordan and he would have another chance to think this through. But he figured if that decision was left to either of them, stopping and rethinking just wasn't in the cards.

He put his phone on the coffee table to free up his hands. Jordan had the same idea, though, because she put aside her phone as well before she hooked her arm around the back of his neck. She pulled him down lower so that the kiss raged on, and she didn't leave things at that. Her other hand went to his chest, and she started to undo the buttons on his shirt.

The memories came. Not of the past two years but of when they'd been lovers. When they'd been very good at what they were doing right now. And his body reacted, all right. Egan got rock hard, and there was a sudden urgency to take this up a notch.

So he did.

He lowered his head to her neck so he could kiss her there, and he went after her buttons, as well. Once he had a few of them open, Egan dropped the kisses lower. To the tops of her breasts. He'd remembered that Jordan liked to be kissed there, and since she reacted with one of those sounds of pleasure, apparently she still did.

The breast kisses put some urgency in her, too, because she started to fight with his shirt. She managed to get it off him, and Jordan must have also remembered where he liked to be kissed because her mouth went to his bare chest. Egan hadn't needed anything else to fire him up, but that did it.

She went lower to his stomach. Another sensitive spot for him. Too sensitive. And he knew if she kept this up that this was all going to end much too fast. That was why he took hold of her, easing her back up so he could take off her top.

Oh, man.

He'd forgotten just what an amazing body she had, but he was sure as heck remembering it now. Remembering even more when he took off her bra, and her breasts spilled into his hands. This time when he pulled her back against him, he had the pleasure of feeling her bare skin against his.

He kissed her mouth again and got her moving toward the bedroom. Thankfully, it was only a few feet away, but even that short distance was enough time for the flames to rise even higher. Yeah, this was wrong, but Egan suddenly wanted her more than his next breath.

And speaking of breaths, Jordan pretty much took his away when she slid her hand over the front of his jeans. Touching him. Reminding him that it had moved from the "want" stage to the "need," and what he needed was Jordan.

He stripped off her top, all the while backing her toward the bed. Still kissing and touching, they fell into a heap on the soft mattress. All in all, the alignment was darn good considering he landed on top of her, and he went after the zipper on her jeans. Egan succeeded with the zipper, but when he went to slide the jeans off her hips, he felt something he didn't want to feel.

Jordan went stiff.

Egan immediately stopped and looked down at her. Her face was flushed with arousal, her breath gusting from her mouth.

"The scar," she said.

This crazy need for her had obviously dulled his mind because it took Egan a couple of seconds to figure out what she meant. She had a scar from her kidney surgery, and it was clearly visible now that he had her partly naked. She'd figured that the scar would remind him of Shanna.

And it did.

But it wasn't a reminder that cooled down his body enough to stop this. He hoped Jordan would feel the same since he was aching to have her.

With Jordan staring at him, Egan waited. Not long, though. She muttered a single word of profanity, slipped her hand around his neck again and pulled him back to a long, deep kiss. Egan was sure he would have felt some relief if she hadn't slid her hand into the waist of his jeans. No relief. Just a higher notch for the heat and need.

Egan did something about her jeans. It wasn't easy with her kissing him, but he finally managed to get them off her. Her panties, too. And he got another jolt of just how beautiful she was. He managed a single kiss on her stomach before Jordan flipped him onto his back so she could rid him of his jeans.

Years ago, they'd had sex in this very room. This very bed. Neither of them had known what they were doing then. It hadn't mattered, though. The only thing that had mattered was satisfying that hunger for each other. Just like now.

Egan took a condom from his wallet before she peeled off his jeans and boxers, but Jordan played a little dirty. She kissed him as she made her way up his body. Egan was already primed and ready, and that didn't help. However, it did feel darn good.

They switched positions again, and he tried to be mindful of her injury. Jordan wanted no part of gentleness, though, because she took hold of his hips and pulled him to her. Until he was deep inside her.

Exactly where he wanted to be.

Egan stilled for a moment just to give her body time to adjust to him. Like the hot, melting kisses, it didn't last, either. The need took over, and he began to move inside her. Jordan moved, too, meeting him thrust for thrust.

Yes, he remembered this, too. The way they'd always fit together. And the fit was just as good now. Maybe too good. Because it didn't last. He felt Jordan's climax ripple through her. Through him, as well. Even though he tried to hang on as long as he could, he knew he couldn't. Egan pushed into her one last time, and he let himself go with her.

Chapter Fourteen

Jordan was afraid to even breathe for fear that Egan would move off her. She wanted to hang on to this close contact with him for as long as possible. Especially since they might not ever be together like this again.

The thought of that twisted away at her, but she had to be realistic. Egan might never be able to forgive her or get past what had happened to Shanna. In fact, he could already be regretting this.

Or not.

He lifted his head, looking down at her, and he kissed her. That certainly didn't seem like something a man with regrets might do. He pushed her hair from her face, continuing to stare at her before he groaned. Now the regrets would come. Except they didn't. He kissed her again, rolled off her and then headed for the bathroom.

"I've got work to do," he added in a grumble.

That was true, but she still wasn't convinced that Egan would use work as a way of distancing himself from her.

She sat up, watching him as he went into the bathroom, and she got a great look at his backside. She wasn't sure how the man managed to look good from all angles, but he did.

Since she didn't want to be sitting around stark naked when Egan returned, Jordan forced herself to get up, and she started to gather her clothes. They were scattered all over the floor so it took her a couple of moments to do it, and she was still dressing when Egan came out of the bathroom. He was still butt naked, which gave her a good look at the front of him.

Yes, definitely great from all angles.

The corner of his mouth lifted as if he'd known what she was thinking, and he began to pick up his clothes. However, he didn't start dressing until he went to her and kissed her again.

"Just in case you're having doubts about this," he drawled.

Well, she certainly didn't have doubts with that chrome-melting kiss, but Jordan figured the postorgasmic glow would wear off soon for both of them. Then reality would put things in perspective. They had a killer after them, too many suspects, few answers and, as Egan had already pointed out, they had work to do.

Egan continued to dress as he made his way back into the living room, and he cursed when he got to his phone on the coffee table. "I have a missed call from Court," he grumbled.

Jordan groaned. She hadn't heard it ring, which was probably the best argument for them not to have landed in bed. Now she only hoped that Court hadn't been in some kind of immediate danger that would have required Egan's help. If he had, then there was no way Egan or she would forgive themselves for that.

Egan put the call on speaker as soon as Court answered. "Are you okay?" Court immediately asked. "I was worried when you didn't answer."

"I'm fine." Egan's jaw was so tight she was surprised he could speak. "What about you?"

"Better than I was about fifteen minutes ago. We got some good news for a change."

Jordan released the breath she'd been holding and went closer to Egan so she could hear Court better.

"The dead guy at the ranch is Donald Brawley," Court continued a moment later. "His prints were in the system because he has two priors. One was an arrest that happened at a chop shop, and it was owned by the same guy who built the custom truck where Kirk was found."

She doubted that was a coincidence, and judging from the sound Egan made, he didn't believe it was one, either.

"But the chop shop arrest is just for starters," Court went on. "Donald is on Leeroy's payroll. He's been working as a ranch hand for him for the past two years."

Jordan's first reaction was relief because they finally had a solid connection that Egan could use to make an arrest. But it didn't take her long to look at this from a different angle. If Leeroy was going to do a murder for hire, then he probably wouldn't have used someone with such a strong link back to him. That was probably why Egan groaned and scrubbed his hand over his face.

"I've already requested financials on Donald," Court explained. "But I'm figuring this was a cash transaction."

"Yeah, but maybe Leeroy got stupid and sloppy and withdrew a large amount of cash in the past forty-eight hours."

"We can only hope. In the meantime I'll have Dakota go out to Leeroy's place and question the other hands there. Dakota'll be able to do that as soon as he finishes with the CSIs at the ranch."

Jordan hadn't even known the reserve deputy was nearby, but it made sense. With a sniper still at large, the CSIs would have wanted police protection while they processed the scene.

"Is Leeroy still there at the station?" Egan asked.

"No. He left a couple of minutes ago after Griff took his statement."

Too bad because if Leeroy had still been in the building, Court could have detained him while they searched for more evidence surrounding his dead employee.

"I can get Leeroy back in here if you want," Court offered.

Egan stayed quiet a moment as if giving that some thought. "Not yet. I'd rather not alert him that we've got an ID on the dead guy. His other ranch hands might clam up and not talk to Dakota if they find out their boss could be a murder suspect."

True. Maybe one of them saw or heard something that they would spill to a deputy.

Egan ended the call, looked up at her, and that was when she saw the regret over what they'd done. At least she thought that was what she was seeing, but Egan shook his head. "We're distractions for each other," he said.

Yes, they were, and he was talking about the missed phone call now. It hadn't been time sensitive, but it could have easily been.

Jordan was about to make the offer to shut herself up in the bedroom. That way, they could work in separate parts of the house. That wouldn't stop her from thinking about him, of course, since in Egan's case, out of sight would not be out of mind. Still, it might help them focus. However, his phone rang before she could even get a chance to suggest it.

"Dakota," Egan said, glancing at the screen.

Since Court had just mentioned the deputy, she thought maybe Dakota was calling to verify that he could indeed go out to Leeroy's, but the way Egan's forehead bunched up, something could be wrong. Since he hadn't put the call on speaker, she went closer, hoping to find out what'd happened.

"What the hell does she want?" Egan snapped.

That question definitely caused Jordan's concern to spike. So did Egan's response several moments later after he listened to whatever it was Dakota said. "They're sure?" Egan asked. A few seconds passed before he groaned and added. "No. I'll talk to her. But I want you to come to the guesthouse to stay with Jordan while I do that."

Egan ended the call, looked at her, and Jordan was certain he was about to tell her something she didn't want to hear. "Is it Tori? Is she here at the ranch?"

He nodded. "She's at the cattle gate, and she told the hands guarding it that she needs to see me, that it's important. She says she'll only talk to me in person. The hands frisked her, and she's not armed. But it appears she has been injured. There are possible stun gun marks on her neck."

Since a stun gun left distinctive marks, it wouldn't have been hard for someone to recognize what they were. But that didn't mean Tori had been attacked. She could have put the marks there herself as some sort of ruse to draw them out into the open.

And it was working.

Well, it was unless she could talk Egan out of going out there.

"This could be a trap," she reminded him. "The sniper could be nearby."

He gave another nod. "I'll stay in the cruiser, and I won't let her anywhere near you."

Jordan shook her head. "It's you that I'm worried about."

"I'll be fine," he assured her, but the heavy sigh that left his mouth suggested otherwise. "We have to get to the bottom of this, and Tori might have the answers we need."

She couldn't argue with the part about Tori having answers, but whether the woman would actually give them to Egan was anyone's guess. Still, she couldn't fault him for wanting to try this.

It wouldn't take the deputy long to get there. Only minutes. And while they waited, Egan finished buttoning his shirt, adjusted his holster and slid on his Stetson.

When she heard the cruiser pull to a stop in front of the guesthouse, she thought maybe Egan would just walk out. He didn't. He hooked his arm around her waist, pulled her to him and kissed her. It wasn't one of the long, smoldering ones that had led them to bed, but it was a reminder that he was indeed an incredible distraction.

And she was falling in love with him all over again.

Jordan kept that to herself. The timing for spilling news like that couldn't be worse. Plus, Dakota knocked on the door.

"It's me," Dakota called out to them.

Egan disconnected the security system so he could let in the deputy. Dakota was wearing a Kevlar vest, which meant he'd been well aware that the sniper could return. Hopefully, the CSIs were wearing the same kind of protective gear.

"Any signs of trouble?" Egan asked him.

"No. Well, other than Tori. But everything

else is going okay. The medical examiner just arrived with his crew."

Egan made a sound of approval, and he gave Jordan one last look. "Reset the alarm after I leave." He rattled off the code to her. "I won't be long."

She hoped that was true, and while she was hoping, Jordan added that Egan would stay safe. If the sniper had managed to shoot into the main house before, he could do it again, and this time they might not get so lucky.

As Egan had reminded her to do, Jordan reset the security system and went to the window to watch him drive away in the cruiser. From where she was standing, she couldn't see the cattle gate or even the road that led to it, but Dakota would have had line of sight of it from the main house.

"Did the hands check Tori's car trunk to make sure no one was with her?" she asked.

"Yeah." He walked to the window and stood next to her. "You think I should call Court for backup?"

Obviously, Dakota was as uneasy about this as she was, but she had to shake her head about calling Court. If Egan had wanted that, he would have already made sure Dakota called him. But Egan had likely figured that his brother already had his hands full without doing backup. Plus, Dakota was there if something went wrong.

Since it wasn't a good idea for her to stay at the window, Jordan went back to the sofa so she could start searching through her files again. She knew she was on edge, but she didn't know just how much until she gasped when the sound of her phone ringing shot through the room.

She hoped it might be Egan's name on the screen and that he was calling to tell her that he was nixing this plan to talk to Tori. But it wasn't Egan. It was coming from an unknown caller again. Since this was probably Christian, she debated if she wanted to talk to him or not. Her nerves were already right at the surface, and a conversation with him likely wouldn't help that. Still, he might be calling about something important so she hit the answer button.

"Jordan," the caller said. Not Christian. Or if it was, he was using a scrambler to disguise himself. This was the same voice of the person who'd called earlier.

The killer.

"What do you want?" Jordan snapped.

The man laughed. "Ready for some fun?" he taunted.

Before she could even respond to that, Jordan heard something she didn't want to hear. The security alarm went off.

Someone was breaking into the house.

FROM HIS REARVIEW MIRROR, Egan kept watch of the guesthouse until it was out of sight. He hadn't wanted to leave Jordan, but he had to do something to put an end to the danger. Those hired thugs had already come way too close to killing her, and he couldn't risk another attack.

Not that Tori would for certain be able to help him with that.

Still, he had to try.

Egan drove past the main house, glancing at the CSIs who were still at work. It was nearly six pm, past what some would consider normal duty hours. However, the CSIs would stay until the job was done.

The body was still there, but since the medical examiner's van was indeed already in place, it meant they'd be moving it soon.

That didn't exactly mean things would return to normal. However, it was a start.

He soon spotted the silver car on the other side of the cattle gate. The hands had wisely kept the gate closed, which meant Tori couldn't have driven onto the property even if that was what she'd intended to do. She didn't look ready to do that, though. She was leaning against the driver's door, and she had one hand pressed to her neck. Her other hand was on her forehead.

Tori looked up, her attention zooming straight toward him as he drove closer. Egan stopped, but as he'd told Jordan, he didn't get out. Instead, he backed up and angled the cruiser so that the driver's side would be facing Tori. He drew his gun, holding it on his lap in case he needed it, and he lowered the window just enough for her to see him.

"You have to help me," Tori said. She went toward him, stumbling several times, before she caught on to the wrought iron rods that made up the gate. "Someone tried to kill me."

"Welcome to the club," he grumbled.

She flinched as if he had struck her. "You're a cop. People probably try to kill you all the time, but this is a first for me. You need to let me in. You need to put me in protective custody."

Egan had to admit that Tori did look as if someone had attacked her. Her hair was a tangled mess, and her blouse sleeve had been torn. There were also what appeared to be bruises and scrapes on her knees.

"What happened?" Egan asked her.

She glanced around, obviously trying to make sure they weren't about to be attacked. Of course, Tori could be faking that glance, and that was why Egan kept watch, too.

"When I was leaving the sheriff's office, someone was hiding in my car. I didn't see the person until it was too late, and he used a stun gun on me." Tori turned to show him the marks on her neck.

"Interesting. That's almost identical to what Kirk said happened to him," Egan commented.

Tory's eyes widened, and a quick burst of breath left her mouth. "Kirk was hurt, too?"

Egan studied her to see if she was truly surprised, but he couldn't tell. "He's at the hospital now."

He wouldn't mention that Kirk might not

make it. If Tori was genuinely shocked, hearing that might make her hysterical, and he might not get any information from her.

"Did the same person attack both of us?" she asked.

Egan lifted his shoulder. "I'm still trying to work that out. Did you get a good look at the person who used the stun gun on you?"

"No. He was wearing a ski mask. It happened so fast, and then he clubbed me on the head. I didn't black out, but I couldn't move. I could hear, though."

Again, that was similar to what'd happened to Kirk except Kirk had then been shot. "Did the man say anything or threaten you?"

"Not that I can recall. Like I said, it happened fast. But I think he was about to shoot me when he heard someone." She touched her fingers to her head as if she was trying to recall something. "I think the guy got spooked. Maybe because Kirk called out to him?" She looked at Egan again. "Was Kirk there, or did I imagine he was?"

"I have no idea." But it was possible that it was indeed Kirk if he was the person behind this. Maybe he'd set it all up, and then one of his hired thugs had turned on him.

But why would Kirk have wanted to hurt Tori?

They'd seemed pretty chummy when they'd been at his office, and Tori had mentioned she'd been staying at Kirk's house. Maybe Kirk hadn't intended for things to go this far. Still, there was something about this that didn't make sense.

"If you honestly thought your life was in danger, why come here?" Egan asked her. "Why not go back to the sheriff's office or the hospital?"

"Once I could move, I knew I had to get out of there. I was afraid the guy with the stun gun would come back to finish me off. So, I started driving, and I ended up here."

Egan was even more skeptical now. "How'd you know this was the McCall Ranch and that I'd be here?"

"I'd looked it up when I first thought someone might be trying to kill me." She paused, her mouth trembling. "I thought maybe you were the one who wanted me dead."

Jordan had thought that, too. At first. She

didn't feel that way now, and that was because of their…well, relationship. If that was indeed what they had. One thing was for certain, he no longer felt the same about Jordan as he had two days ago, and he could partly blame the sex for that. Sex had a way of ripping down barriers. And clouding his mind.

Like now.

Tori was clearly still a suspect. Maybe she'd been a victim or she could be just playing the part. Either way, it was obvious he wasn't going to get what he needed from her.

"Wait here," Egan told Tori, "and I'll have a couple of the hands follow you back into town. I want you to go to the hospital so your injuries can be checked."

And that way, Egan could get a report back from the doctor so he could figure out if her injuries were self-induced.

"I don't want to wait here," she protested. Her grip tightened on the gate. "It's dangerous. I want to go with you."

No way would that happen, but he had a sickening feeling that Tori might be trying to stall him. And there was only one reason she would do something like that.

Hell.

Egan glanced back at the medical examiner's van and the other two cars that the CSIs had almost certainly used to get onto the ranch. "Did either of you search those vehicles?" he asked the hands.

The hands both shook their heads, causing Egan to curse. Tori called out for him to stop, but he ignored her. He turned the cruiser around as fast as he could, hit the accelerator and sped toward the guesthouse.

He kept watch in his rearview mirror to make sure that Tori didn't try to get past the gate or attack one of the hands. She didn't. She appeared to be cursing at him when she hurried back to her car and got inside. Egan slowed just enough to make sure she wasn't going to ram into the gate, but instead she drove out in as much of a hurry as Egan was.

His pulse was pounding by the time he braked to a stop on the side of the guesthouse behind Dakota's cruiser. He got his weapon ready, stepped out and immediately heard something.

The security alarm.

It was clanging, which meant something or someone had triggered one of the sensors. He figured it was too much to hope that Jordan or Dakota had accidently set it off.

And then he saw something else from the corner of his eye that confirmed that this wasn't a false alarm.

He saw the man climbing through the bedroom window.

Egan took aim and fired. But it was too late. The man was inside the house.

Chapter Fifteen

Jordan had gotten her gun the moment she heard the security alarm go off, but the alarm was also masking other sounds that she needed to hear.

Like the specific location of the intruder.

Dakota readied his gun, too, and they both fired gazes around the guest cottage, looking for any signs of what was going on. Nothing. Well, nothing until the thick blast from someone firing a shot outside.

That caused her heart to jump to her throat, and she hurried to the security keypad so she could turn off the alarm. That was when she heard the sound of hurried footsteps coming from the bedroom. The door was open, and she pivoted in that direction.

But it was too late.

A man was already there. Someone whom

she didn't recognize, and he had his gun aimed. Not at her but rather at Dakota.

The thug pulled the trigger before either Dakota or she could, and the shot slammed into the deputy's chest. Dakota made a sharp sound of pain and dropped to the floor.

Jordan knew the bulletproof vest had probably stopped it from being a fatal shot, but it had obviously knocked the breath out of him. The next one could kill him if she didn't do something to prevent it from happening. Since the gunman was also wearing Kevlar, it meant she had to go for a head shot.

Jordan was about to fire, but the man lunged at her. There were only a few feet of space between them, and that was gone within a split second when he crashed into her and knocked her gun from her hand. They both went to the floor with the back of her head slamming against the door. It hit so hard that the pain shot through her, and her vision blurred. Not good. Because she needed to be able to see her attacker to try to stop him.

Her attacker obviously had no trouble seeing her, though. He bashed his elbow right into her chin, causing her head to slam against the door again. This time, it was more than just blurry vision. She saw the dark spots and knew that she was about to lose consciousness.

"Jordan?" someone called out.

Egan. He was close. Right outside from the sound of it, and it made her wonder if he'd been the one to fire the shot she'd heard. Of course, it could have been this goon shooting at Egan, and if so, she prayed he was all right. Dakota, too. The deputy was alive, but he was clutching his chest and moaning in pain.

The man hit her again with his elbow when she tried to reach back for the doorknob. This blow was the hardest yet, and she was surprised that it hadn't broken her jaw. It only added to the god-awful pain she was already feeling.

She fought to stay alert. And tried to fight the thug, too, but he outweighed her by a good fifty pounds. Jordan latched on to him with the only weapon she had. She sank her teeth into his hand and bit down with every ounce of energy she could muster.

The thug howled in pain and punched her again. That stopped her, temporarily, but she would have gone back for a second assault if he hadn't caught on to her hair. He grabbed a huge handful, and he dragged her to her feet.

He put the gun to her head just as Egan threw open the door.

"Watch out!" Jordan tried to warn him.

But it was already too late. The thug turned his gun in Egan's direction. And he fired. Thankfully, Egan jumped out of the way in the nick of time, and he landed on the ground just to the side of the door.

Since the thug's gun was right against her ear, the shot, and the one that followed, was deafening. The sound roared through her head and made the pain even worse. But she tried to push the fear and pain aside so she could help Egan. That was hard to do, though, because her attacker had her in a choke hold.

Egan glanced around the corner of the door and lifted his gun. He cursed, though, probably because he realized he didn't have a clean shot. Her attacker was using her as a human shield. Plus, if Egan leaned out too far, he would make an easy target, and this time the thug might not miss.

She could hear Dakota groaning. The deputy was still on the floor, still trying to catch his breath. But if he managed that, he might be able to pick up his gun that had fallen to the floor and use it to stop the man before someone got killed.

"Did Tori send you?" she managed to ask the man.

Jordan didn't expect him to answer, and he didn't. That didn't mean Tori was innocent, and the timing of her visit was certainly suspicious. The woman could have used her arrival as a distraction so that her hired gun could break into the house. The goon might not have tried something like that if Egan had been inside. And Jordan was certain that Egan was cursing himself about that.

"I've already called for backup," Egan told the man. "Let Jordan go."

"Not a chance. She's coming with me." And with the choke hold even tighter now, he started backing up toward the rear door that was just off the kitchen.

Maybe the man had someone out there waiting to help him. Or he could have a vehicle he could use to escape with her. Yes, the hands had been keeping watch, but that didn't mean someone couldn't have gotten past them.

Egan continued to make glances around the door. No doubt looking for an opening so he could shoot. Jordan doubted the hired gun was going to allow such an opening, so she looked around for anything she could use to help fight him off. There was a wooden block with knives on the kitchen counter, but they were out of her reach. The only other thing was a coffee cup.

So, that was what Jordan grabbed.

She figured she had only a few seconds at most, so the moment she had it in her grip, she threw her weight against the man. In the same motion, she raised the cup and bashed it against the side of his head.

He cursed her and immediately tried to jostle her back into his choke hold. Jordan dropped down, sliding right out of his grasp. She didn't take the time to get her footing. She just started running toward the front door, and the moment she reached it, she went out and ducked to the side as Egan had done.

Egan was crouched down with a tight grip on his gun, but he used his left hand to sling her behind him. So that he was in front and protecting her. Jordan didn't want his protection, though, if it meant he was going to take a bullet for her.

And the bullet came, all right.

It bashed into the door frame, tearing off a chunk of the wood. The second one did even more damage.

"Keep watch behind us," Egan told her.

That sent her pulse skyrocketing. Of course, she'd known this thug might not have come alone, but she didn't want Egan and her to be ambushed.

Egan took out his backup weapon from the sliding holster in his jeans and handed it to her. Good. At least now she had a way to try to defend them. Thankfully, though, there didn't seem to be anyone else around them, though she could see the CSIs peering around the side of the main house. They'd no doubt heard the shots and were looking to see if they could help.

Jordan motioned for them to stay back, and she turned, ready to help Egan with the hired gun. But the shots stopped. Egan cursed again, and since she couldn't see into the guesthouse, she wasn't sure what had caused his reaction. Or why his muscles suddenly went even stiffer than they already were.

"Backup plan," the thug growled. And he laughed.

She risked peering around the jamb then,

and her stomach went to her knees. That was because Dakota was no longer on the floor. Just as the thug had done to her, he now had Dakota in front of him.

"You'll be coming with me," the thug said, looking directly at Jordan. "Or else Deputy Cowboy gets a bullet to the head."

FROM THE MOMENT that Egan had seen the gunman and the situation in the guesthouse, he'd known it could come down to this. He'd just hoped, though, that he could stop the snake before anyone got hurt.

But someone was already hurt.

Dakota had a chest injury probably from a bullet that this jerk had fired into his bulletproof vest. Jordan's face was bruised and bleeding, and she was clearly in pain. Enough pain that forced Egan to rein in his temper. If he didn't, he was going to rush inside and tear that idiot gunman limb from limb. He couldn't risk doing that because he could be shot. That would leave Dakota and Jordan even more vulnerable than they already were.

And they were already plenty vulnerable enough.

He didn't even know what they were up

against. If his theory was right about the gunman getting onto the ranch in the ME's van, then he could have brought several hired thugs with him. Maybe the person behind this had come as well, with the plan to finish them all off.

Egan glanced behind him at the CSIs. They weren't armed, so hopefully they'd stay behind cover. Maybe Court would arrive soon, too. Egan had texted him right before he'd unlocked the guesthouse door. But even if Court did get there in record time, he didn't want his brother walking into the middle of what could easily turn out to be a gunfight.

"Well?" the thug snarled. "Are you just gonna cower there and let the deputy die?"

The question and the attitude were no doubt meant to draw Jordan out. And it just might work, too. That was why Egan stayed in front of her. He considered asking her to use her former hostage-negotiating skills, but he didn't want her to engage in conversation with his moron. Jordan was almost certainly thinking about her last hostage situation. One where Shanna had been killed. This thug would play on that grief and use it to try to kill her.

"If you shoot the deputy," Egan tossed back

at him, "you'll lose your human shield, and I'll blow your brains out. You're sure you're ready to die for your boss?"

Egan glanced around the doorjamb and saw that the guy's jaw had turned to iron. Good. Egan wanted to keep pushing at any hot button he could find.

"Did your boss pay you enough to die?" Egan added. He adjusted his stance in case he had to fire. No way could he surrender or give in to this guy's demands. Because Egan was certain the thug's orders were to kill Jordan and him. Then he'd kill Dakota so there wouldn't be any witnesses.

"I can match whatever your boss is paying you," Egan went on. "And give you a sweet deal to cut down on your jail time."

The last part was an out-and-out lie. Even if he could have, he wouldn't have made that kind of deal and let a killer or would-be killer walk. Egan suspected, though, that this guy fell into the killer category. He'd likely been the one to kill at least one of the recipients.

But why?

Egan still didn't have an answer to that.

"Shut up," the man finally snapped. "And get the woman out here right now."

He jammed his gun even harder against Dakota's head, and the deputy winced. Dakota also made direct eye contact with Egan, maybe a way of letting him know that he'd regained enough of his breath to do something to stop this.

"The woman's not going anywhere." Egan made sure there was no doubt whatsoever about that in his tone.

The guy's jaw got even tighter, and he began to fire some nervous glances around the room. Maybe trying to decide if he should just cut his losses and try to escape with Dakota. But obviously Dakota had a different notion about having that play out. The deputy lifted his left eyebrow, and even though Egan didn't know exactly what he had in mind, he got ready.

Just as Dakota jabbed his elbow into the guy's gut.

Coughing and cursing, the man staggered back. And he pulled the trigger of his gun. Egan wasn't sure where the shot went, but he didn't waste any time. He charged into the guesthouse and tackled the thug before he could get off another shot.

The momentum of his body and speed sent

both the thug and him crashing against the fridge. Egan managed to hold on to his gun, but so did the thug. He tried to bring it up so he could shoot Egan, but he put a stop to that by head-butting the idiot. He'd have a helluva headache later, but it'd be worth it because the impact knocked the guy against the fridge again.

This time, Egan disarmed him. And he punched him.

"That's payback for what you did to Jordan and Dakota," Egan growled. "I need some plastic cuffs," he added to Dakota.

While Dakota was getting those from his pocket, Egan turned the thug, shoving him face-first against the fridge. He wasn't easy with him when he put on the cuffs, but then this idiot hadn't been easy with Jordan or Dakota.

Once he had him restrained, Egan put him belly-down on the floor, the best position to make sure he didn't try to escape. Egan wanted him alive. And talking. He wanted to know the name of the person who'd hired him to create this hellish nightmare.

But the nightmare wasn't over.

Egan's heart slammed against his chest when he looked in the doorway to check on Jordan.

Damn.

She wasn't alone. There was a man wearing a ski mask directly behind her. And he'd taken her hostage.

Chapter Sixteen

Jordan couldn't breathe. The man holding her was choking her as he moved back from the door with her.

But she didn't need her breath to silently curse herself for getting into a position like this. She should have been paying closer attention to her surroundings, but instead she'd been focused on keeping her gun aimed at the thug whom Egan was arresting. She hadn't wanted him to try to fight his way out this situation and hurt Egan or Dakota in the process.

Now she was paying for her lapse in judgment.

Unfortunately, though, Egan and Dakota might have to pay, too.

Both of them immediately took cover, which meant they were out of the line of fire, but she doubted that would last. Egan probably wouldn't just stand by while she was in danger. But she wished he would. Jordan wished that he would stay put and save himself and his deputy. Because if he came out after her, he'd be an easy target for this snake who had her.

Unlike the hired gun who'd shot Dakota, this one didn't say anything to Egan. He just started dragging her toward Egan's cruiser. It wasn't far, only a couple of yards away, which meant it wouldn't take him long to get her there and inside.

His choke hold was so tight that Jordan wasn't even sure she could speak loud enough for the goon to hear her, but she tried anyway. "How did you get on the ranch?"

In the grand scheme of things, it wasn't important for her to know the answer, but she wanted to hear him speak so she could try to recognize his voice. If he was a stranger, just another hired gun, maybe then she could try to bargain with him by offering to pay him more than his boss was paying him. That hadn't worked with the goon inside the house, but she had to try.

"He came in the ME's van," she heard Egan say. He was no longer in the kitchen but rather to the side of the doorway. "He knew the van would be coming to the ranch, and he used it to sneak onto the grounds."

The man certainly didn't deny that.

Egan stepped out even farther into the doorway, and she prayed if this man turned his gun on him that Egan would at least get down.

"Take me instead of Jordan," Egan bargained. Jordan shook her head to nix that. Or rather she tried. But the man held on, and he didn't stop until he had her right next to the cruiser.

"You think it's smart to start driving off with Jordan?" Egan continued. With a firm grip on his gun, he came out into the yard. "She's a former cop. She'll fight you. And if you wreck, it could kill both of you."

For the first time since the man had taken her, she felt some hesitation. He didn't reach for the door. He stood there a moment staring at Egan.

"Get behind the wheel," the man said. Like the phone calls, it wasn't a normal voice. He was using some kind of scrambler. Maybe a small one hidden beneath the ski mask.

"No," Jordan managed to say. She definitely didn't want Egan coming with them because it would be a death sentence. But her "no" didn't do a thing to stop him.

"Drop your gun on the ground," the man ordered.

Now it was Egan's turn to hesitate, and she knew why. She had his backup gun. Or rather she'd had it before this thug had knocked it from her hand and taken her captive. Now, if Egan surrendered his primary, he wouldn't have a weapon that he could use to fight back.

Egan's hesitation didn't last long, and her heart sank when he tossed his gun on the ground and started for the cruiser. She braced herself in case the goon tried to kill him, but he didn't. With her neck still in his tight grip, he stepped back so that Egan could open the door, and he got behind the wheel. The man then shoved her into the back seat and followed right behind her. He didn't waste any time putting the gun back to her head.

"Drive," he told Egan.

Dakota came to the door of the guesthouse, and the deputy looked ready to come after them, but Egan waved him off and started the engine. Even though Jordan didn't want to be at the mercy of this snake, she also didn't want the deputy hurt or killed. If Dakota tried to get to them, that would almost certainly happen.

Egan's phone rang. Perhaps it was Court or one of the hands or CSIs trying to figure out what was going on, but Egan didn't answer it.

"Where to?" Egan asked as he put on his seat belt.

He met her gaze in the rearview mirror, and it wasn't hard to tell what he was thinking. Egan was blaming himself for this. But it wasn't his fault. Nor was it hers. Jordan put the blame for this solely on the shoulders of the man who now had them at gunpoint.

Since she'd been a cop, she knew how plenty of situations like these played out. If their captor could manage to get them to a secondary location, it would be easier for him to kill them. Probably the only reason he hadn't done that at the guesthouse was because he wouldn't have had an escape. This way he did, which meant he probably intended to kill them as soon as he had them off the ranch.

"Just drive," the man snarled. "When you get to the gate, make sure your hands back off or they'll die. Then get the gate open."

Egan had a remote to do that, but maybe the man didn't know that. A remote would just get them off the ranch faster, and maybe Egan could claim he needed to get out of the vehicle to open it. Of course, he wouldn't use that opportunity to get away, but maybe he could at least get himself out of the line of fire. That might give Court time to arrive so he could help them put a stop to this.

When Egan started driving, Jordan looked back at the CSIs. They were armed now, maybe with weapons they'd gotten from the house. But like the ranch hands, they were unable to do anything for fear their captor would kill them. Or rather one of them anyway. Jordan figured she was the expendable one now, and it sickened her to think that she might die and not even know the reason why.

The person under the ski mask could be another hired gun. One working for Leeroy or even Kirk if his thugs had indeed gone rogue. Or the man's boss could be Tori, who was working on behalf of Drew. She couldn't rule out their other suspect, either—Christian.

"Why are you doing this?" she asked.

He didn't answer, of course. He just kept the gun on her while he watched every move that Egan made. She felt his hand tense, though, when Egan approached the gate.

That was probably because of the two armed hands there.

"Call them," the man said to Egan. "Tell them to stand down."

Egan took out his phone and did that, and she watched as the hands hesitantly lowered their guns and stepped back off the road and away from the gate. Egan looked at her again in the mirror, and it seemed as if he was trying to tell her something. Exactly what, though, she didn't know, but Jordan tried to brace herself for whatever it was he was about to do.

She didn't have to wait long.

Without warning, Egan slammed his foot on the accelerator, crashing the cruiser into the iron gate.

EGAN HAD KNOWN the crash was a huge risk, but everything he did at this point would be. But the biggest risk of all would have been to allow this thug to get Jordan and him off the ranch. This way, he at least had some backup if he managed to get her out of the cruiser.

That was a big *if*, though.

Egan was wearing his seat belt, and when he'd made the call to the hands, he'd turned off the airbag so that it wouldn't punch him in the face. But Jordan and the thug holding her weren't strapped in so they went flying into the back of the seat. Exactly what Egan had wanted. Now he only had to hope and pray that Jordan didn't get hurt worse than she already was.

The man cursed, the words still filtered through the scrambler, and he regained his balance a little sooner than Egan had wanted. He also managed to hang on to his gun. Still, Egan came over the seat after him. He needed to pin the guy long enough for Jordan to escape.

"Get out of here," Egan shouted to her. "Run!" And he launched himself at the man.

Egan tackled him, trying to pin him to the seat, but he didn't manage to do that before the idiot pulled the trigger. The shot blasted through the cruiser, and Egan prayed the sound of pain that Jordan made was because it hurt her ears and not because she'd been shot. He couldn't check on her, though, because Egan was suddenly in the fight for their lives.

The man bashed his gun so hard against Egan's head that he was certain he'd have a concussion. Still, that didn't stop him. Egan swung his fist and managed to connect with the guy's jaw. His head flopped back, but he managed to get off another shot.

Worse, Jordan was still in the cruiser.

Egan wanted to shout at her again to get out, but she started hitting the thug on the head. It wasn't doing much to deter him, though, because he fired a third time, and he latched on to Jordan, dragging her against him. He was going to use her as a human shield again if Egan didn't do something to stop it.

From the corner of his eye, Egan saw the hands move closer. They both had their guns aimed, but there was no way they had a clean shot because Jordan was between the hands and the thug.

Jordan kept clawing at the man, and everything seemed to go still when she ripped the ski mask off his face. Egan had expected to be staring down at another hired gun. But he wasn't.

It was Christian.

Jordan gasped and then froze for a split second. It was just enough time for Christian to grab her again and put the gun to her head.

"I won't miss at point-blank range," Christian growled, and he used his left hand to yank the voice scrambler pressed to his throat.

No, Christian wouldn't miss, and the look in the man's eyes told Egan everything he needed to know. Christian was going to kill them.

And Egan knew why.

"You're a dirty cop," Egan snapped. "And you were afraid Jordan would uncover the evidence in those files she had."

Christian certainly didn't deny it. "Get behind the wheel again, and you'd better pray you didn't damage the cruiser so much that you can't drive it. If you did, I start putting bullets in Jordan. The shots won't be fatal, but she'll be in so much pain that she'll wish she was dead."

It wasn't a bluff. Christian would do it, and Egan wasn't sure he could watch another woman he cared about be gunned down right in front of him. He fought to keep the flashbacks at bay, but it was hard to do.

Hell. He could lose Jordan.

"Drive!" Christian shouted.

Egan didn't have a choice. He climbed back over the seat and hoped he got another chance to stop this piece of dirt from doing any more harm.

Thankfully, the cruiser engine was still running, but Egan didn't know if the engine had been damaged or not. He might not make it far, and he'd almost certainly meet Court along the way. He had to make sure his brother didn't get hurt while trying to save them. His first priority, though, was to get Jordan out of this. She was no doubt Christian's primary target. The only reason the cop wanted Egan dead was probably because he knew Jordan had talked to him about what she'd uncovered in those files.

Too bad that Egan hadn't let someone else know. That way, if Christian did manage to murder them and get away, then his brother and Griff could go after him. Egan wasn't even sure the hands had gotten a good enough look at Christian's face to ID him.

This time, Egan used the remote to open the gate, and he kept watch of Christian and Jordan while he waited for it to slide open. Christian would be ready if Egan tried to crash the vehicle again so he couldn't do that. However, he could watch for some kind of opening for him to stop this.

"You killed all those people to cover up what you did," Jordan said. Her voice was trembling, but she managed to glare at the man.

"I did what I had to do," Christian mumbled.

"No, you did that to save yourself from the death penalty," she fired back. "People died, and two men are on death row because of you."

"Those men deserved it. They weren't angels. They were just as deep in the operation as I was."

The *operation* in this case was human trafficking. And yeah, there'd been deaths associated with both cases.

"I'm guessing the men on death row didn't know you'd honchoed both the human trafficking and their arrests," Egan commented.

He watched Christian's expression in the mirror and was pleased when he saw the raw anger in the cop's eyes. Maybe he could goad Christian into turning his gun on him instead of Jordan.

When the gate was finally open, Egan drove through it and onto the road that would take him to the highway. He spotted Court's truck, making his way toward them, and he knew he didn't have much time.

"I'm guessing Leeroy and Kirk didn't have anything to do with this," Egan continued. "But you're working for Tori, right? She's the one who put all of this together. She's definitely got more brains than you do."

No way did Egan believe that, but it got the reaction he wanted. Another flash of anger went through Christian's eyes.

"I'm the one holding Jordan," Christian practically yelled. "I'm the one cleaning up my own mess. That bimbo lawyer didn't have anything to do with this. In fact, if I hadn't gotten the wrong woman, she'd be dead by now."

So, Lorena's death had been a mistake. That wouldn't bring much comfort to her grieving family, and Christian didn't seem the least bit concerned that he'd murdered a woman who'd had no part in this.

Egan rarely put the cold-blooded-killer label on anyone, but it fit Christian to a T. Worse, he was a cop, and he'd used his badge to help him commit these crimes.

"You're the one who left that note with Lorena's body?" Egan asked.

"Of course!" Christian snapped. "But that doesn't matter now. None of that matters."

Court stopped his truck at the turn from the highway to the ranch road, and Egan knew his brother was preparing to fight back. That meant Egan had to do something now. He just prayed that the *something* he was about to do was right.

When he was only about ten yards from Court, Egan jerked the steering wheel to the right and sent the cruiser straight into the ditch. It was like hitting a brick wall, and this time Egan wasn't wearing his seat belt. He slammed into the steering wheel, the pain shooting through him, but he ignored it and barreled over the seat again.

Christian was ready for him.

But Egan was ready, too.

Christian had turned the gun on him, but Egan crashed right into him before the man could pull the trigger. Egan grabbed hold of Christian's right wrist, pinning his shooting hand and the gun against the window. But Christian didn't exactly surrender. The cop used his left fist to punch Egan.

Jordan fought, too. She latched on to Christian's arm to try to stop him from hitting

Egan again, but the rage and adrenaline fueled Christian so that he could easily throw her off. Jordan landed hard against the cruiser door, and Egan figured that would only add more injuries to the ones Christian had already given her.

The thought of that gave Egan his own surge of rage and adrenaline. Egan couldn't pry the man's grip off his gun, and he managed to get his own hand in a position to bash the weapon against Christian's head. Christian cursed him and kept fighting, but Egan continued to hit him with the gun. Egan had so much anger in him that he hoped he bashed his brains out.

The cruiser door flew open, and Egan got a glimpse of Court. His brother had his weapon raised, but like the hands he didn't have a clean shot. Egan tried to do something about that.

While Egan continued to hit Christian, he also tried to push Jordan out of the cruiser. She wouldn't budge, though, and she managed to land some hard blows to the side of Christian's face.

Until Christian pulled the trigger.

The fear slammed into Egan as hard as the

adrenaline had, and he pinpointed all of that into one last effort to stop this snake. Egan rammed the gun not against Christian's head but to his throat.

Finally.

Christian made a garbled sound as he fought for his breath, and he relaxed his grip on the gun just enough for Egan to take hold of it. He immediately pointed it at Christian.

"Please move so I can kill you," Egan warned him. And it wasn't a bluff. More than anything he wanted this man to pay for what he'd done.

Well, almost more than anything.

He needed Jordan to be okay, but Egan was almost afraid to look at her. When he did, his stomach went into a knot. There was blood on her face, and she looked as if she'd been beaten to a pulp. But she was alive, thank God, and it didn't appear that Christian had managed to shoot her.

"Go to Court," Egan told her, though he wasn't sure how he managed to speak. It felt as if his throat had clamped shut.

She gave a shaky nod and started to move. But Christian moved, too.

He whipped out a knife from his pocket.

Egan saw the light glint off the shiny metal blade, and he fired at him, the bullet slamming into Christian.

But the damage had already been done.

In that exact second that Egan's bullet was killing him, Christian plunged the knife into Jordan.

Chapter Seventeen

This was a repeat of the nightmare.

Just like the night Shanna had died, Egan could do nothing but pray and pace across the hospital waiting room. Maybe, just maybe, this would have a different outcome.

The images kept replaying in his head. Of Christian jabbing his knife into Jordan. Images of the blood and the color draining from Jordan's face. There'd been no color in Christian's, either, because Egan's shot had killed him, but now the same thing might happen to Jordan.

"You want me to pace for you for a while so you can get some rest?" Court asked him.

Egan appreciated his brother's concern and even Court's half attempt to lighten things up, but no way could he sit down. If he stopped, he might explode. Too bad he didn't have

Christian there in front of him so he had a way to burn off some of this dangerous energy coiled inside him.

Court's phone buzzed, something it'd been doing a lot since they'd arrived at the hospital nearly a half hour earlier. Egan suspected Court was getting updates on the case. Updates that Egan wanted to hear, but first he needed to make sure Jordan was okay, and that wasn't happening.

When they'd arrived, the nurses had immediately whisked Jordan away and had stopped Egan when he tried to follow. He'd argued with them, but then the doctor had come out and said he might need to prep Jordan for surgery. Even that hadn't worked until the doctor had reminded him that the knife wound was in the same area as Jordan's only kidney.

If the kidney was damaged, Jordan might die.

That had finally stopped Egan from trying to follow Jordan, but he was wishing it hadn't. There were things he wanted to say to Jordan, and he might not get a chance to do that.

"Tori's all right," Court relayed when he finished his latest call. "But the marshals are going to put her in protective custody for a while just in case Christian has another hired thug out there somewhere."

That was a good precaution to take, though Egan figured any hired thug would be long gone now that his boss had been killed. There'd be no reason for someone to hang around and risk arrest when there were multiple murder charges involved.

"Thea's questioning Christian's gunman who you caught at the guesthouse, and she's been sending me text updates," Court went on. "The guy's name is Steve Bartow, and he's talking. He says he wants a plea deal."

"He's not getting one," Egan growled.

Court made a sound of agreement. "He claims he didn't kill anyone, that the murders are all on Christian."

He might be saying that to save his own skin, but it didn't matter. Accessory to murder carried the same penalty as murder. "I want him charged with all the deaths and the attacks. If he gives us anything that will tie up any remaining loose ends, I'll consider asking the DA to take the death penalty off the table."

"You think there are any loose ends?" Court asked.

"Not really. I believe Christian might have

even been the sniper who attacked the ranch," Egan added. "As a cop, he certainly had the training to do something like that." And he would have known how to evade an arrest.

It sickened Egan to think that Christian could have been following their every move through legal police channels. That was probably how he'd managed to get to those other women.

Court got another text. "It's from Thea," he said after he read whatever was on the screen. "The talking hired thug said it was Christian who attacked Kirk. Apparently, Christian did that because he thought Kirk and Tori were on to him."

If they were, neither Tori nor Kirk had brought that to Egan. Of course, there'd been a lot of accusations and bogus info thanks to Christian. Maybe he'd let something slip, and Tori and Kirk had figured out he was up to no good. Egan certainly wished he'd figured it out sooner. If he had, Jordan might not have gotten hurt.

The ER doors slid open, and because Egan was still on edge, he automatically put his hand over his gun. And he kept it there when he saw Leeroy come in. Leeroy looked around the room and made a beeline toward Egan when he spotted him.

"I don't have time for your smart mouth and venom," Egan snapped. He expected that to set Leeroy off and have the man launch into a tirade.

He didn't. In fact, Leeroy nodded. "It's all over town that the dirty cop was killing the folks who got Shanna's organs. Is it true?"

"Yeah. He did it so he could murder Jordan to silence her." Just saying that twisted away at him, and it felt as if someone had put his heart in a vise and was squeezing hard. "The other donors were just decoys he used to cover up his real motive."

Leeroy shook his head and muttered something under his breath that Egan didn't catch. "You know I was against Shanna donating her organs, but I never wanted this. I never wanted anyone else to die."

The man sounded genuine, and Egan decided to take him at his word. "Then, you need to back off. Jordan could have a long recovery ahead of her, and she'll need some peace and quiet." He refused to think the worst, that this could end the same way for her as it had for Shanna.

Leeroy nodded. "I won't give her any trouble. Nor Tori." He paused. "I guess you could say this is a truce."

Since they'd been at each other's throats for two years, Egan was suspicious. "Why the change of heart?"

Leeroy stayed quiet a moment. "It was all these people dying and getting hurt. I guess it finally hit me square in the face that I'll never get Shanna back. But I don't wish anyone else any harm. Not even you. I hope Jordan recovers and you two have a happy life together." He tipped his Stetson in a farewell greeting and walked away.

A happy life together?

Egan silently repeated those words to himself, wondering if it was even possible.

"You think hell just froze over?" Court asked.

No. This was more like a mini-miracle. One that Egan would take. He had enough craziness in his life and was glad to have Leeroy out of the mix.

Egan checked his watch again, and he was certain that time had stopped. So had his stash of patience, and he headed in the direction of the examining room where he'd seen the nurses take Jordan. Thankfully, Court didn't even try to stop him. Not that he could have anyway. Because Egan had to know what was going on.

He tried to prepare himself for what he would see. Maybe Jordan would be bleeding. Dying. And there was blood, all right. That was the first thing he noticed when he opened the door. Her blood-soaked shirt was on the table. She was still wearing a bra, but it was bloody, too.

But she wasn't dying, thank God.

In fact, she was sitting up while the nurse stitched up her side. Dr. Madison was there, and she immediately went to him as if to show him right back out. Egan held his ground.

"I have to know how Jordan is," he said with way too much emotion in his voice. He needed to stay calm because Jordan had already had a megadose of fear and emotion today.

"I'm fine," Jordan insisted, and she reached out her hand to him, causing the nurse to scold her for moving. "The knife didn't hit anything vital."

Egan snapped toward the doctor to make

sure that was true, and he released the breath he'd been holding when Dr. Madison nodded.

"She was very lucky. Another inch higher, and…well, she wouldn't be sitting up right now."

An inch. That squeezed at his heart even more. That was how close he'd come to losing her.

When Jordan held out her hand again, he went to her. Egan wanted to pull her into his arms and kiss her. He wanted to hold her and make sure she was okay, but he didn't want to interfere with the stitches. Especially when he got a better look at the wound. It was an angry-looking gash on her rib cage.

"It looks worse than it is," Jordan assured him, and she gave his hand a gentle squeeze.

A nick would have looked bad enough for him right now, especially considering the bruises on her face. He lightly touched the one on her cheekbone, and he felt another jolt of rage for Christian. The idiot had done this to her, and death was too easy of a punishment for him.

"Again, it looks worse than it is," Jordan said when he touched the bruise on her chin.

"How about you? Please tell me yours are worse than they look."

Egan had no idea what she meant until he glanced at himself in the mirror above the sink. Yeah, he was a mess. His lip was busted, and he had plenty of bruises. Again, thanks to Christian.

"He refused medical treatment," the nurse said. Her name was Mildred Jenkins, and Egan had known her his entire life. What he hadn't known was that she was a tattletale.

"I'm okay," he assured Jordan, and that wasn't a lie. Now that he knew her injuries weren't life-threatening, that knot in his stomach had eased up considerably.

"How's Dakota?" Jordan asked.

"Court checked on him shortly after we got here. He's got a cracked rib and a fist-sized bruise on his chest, but he'll be fine."

"And Kirk?"

The news wasn't so good on that front. "He made it through surgery. I'm sure he'll be glad to hear that I no longer consider him a suspect."

"Yes," Jordan said, her voice cracking a little. There it was. More of that emotion that she probably didn't need, but it would be with them for a while. Maybe not a life-time, though.

"In hindsight, the pieces all fit," Egan continued. "Christian orchestrated the murders to cover up his crimes, and he hired some thugs to help him." In this case, thugs whom he hoped to use to implicate others—like Leeroy.

But it hadn't worked.

"His hired thug is talking, by the way," Egan added.

"Good. I don't want any doubts in anyone's mind that Christian was a killer."

No. No doubts. And they didn't have to worry about his trying to launch another attack because he was dead.

"The cases of the men who Christian put in jail will have to be reviewed." Jordan made it sound as if she'd get straight to work on that. She probably would, too. Even after everything she'd been through, she'd want justice for those whom Christian had set up.

Mildred finally finished with the stitches, stepped back and looked Egan straight in the eyes. "When you kiss her, be careful, or you'll pop her stitches and bust open your lip again."

Egan frowned. "Why are you so sure I'm going to kiss her?" He was going to do that, but he'd wondered how Mildred had figured it out.

Mildred gave him an isn't-it-obvious look, patted his arm and walked out.

"I'll see about getting you some pain meds," Dr. Madison added. "And then you can take her home."

Egan had been so sure they'd be keeping Jordan overnight, so this was a gift. It meant she really was okay. Well, physically anyway. He didn't like that troubled look in Jordan's eyes, and that was why he did kiss her as soon as Dr. Madison was out of the room. He kept it gentle.

But Jordan didn't.

She slipped her arm around his waist, pulled him closer and made the kiss much longer and hotter than it should have been. It worked, though, because when she finally stopped the kiss the troubled look was gone, and she was smiling.

"I need to tell you some things," she said before he could speak. Ironic, since he was about to say that he needed to tell her some things, too.

"You saved my life," Jordan went on, "and I'm very thankful for that."

"I wouldn't have needed to save your life if I hadn't left to go talk to Tori. That's when the thug broke into the guesthouse, and he wouldn't have done that had I been there."

"You're wrong. He would have still gotten in, and he would have shot you just as he did Dakota. Except you would have had worse than a cracked rib because you weren't wearing Kevlar."

"I could have maybe stopped the guy from shooting," Egan argued.

He didn't get far with that argument, though, because she kissed him again. And again, it was way too hot. He was pretty sure he busted his lip open again, but he didn't care. He had Jordan in his arms, right where he wanted her.

"Now, on to the next thing I have to tell you," she said. "This is going to make you very uneasy, but I have to say it. I'm in love with you. I've been in love with you for most of my life, and I didn't realize it until today when I almost lost you." She stared at him. "Now you can panic."

Egan was feeling a lot of things, but panic sure as heck wasn't one of them. The knot in his stomach finally eased up. So did the tightness in his chest. And he felt something he hadn't felt in a long time.

Happiness.

Yep, that was what he was feeling, all right.

She kept staring at him as if trying to steel herself up for him to reject her. No way was that going to happen, so he gently pulled her back to him. "You love me?"

Jordan nodded.

"Good. Because I'm in love with you, too, and I don't want to go through another minute of it without letting you know."

She smiled again, and this one was dazzling. Jordan was obviously feeling a little happiness as well because it was all over her face. She caught on to the front of his shirt, wadding it up in her hand as she pulled him down for another kiss. It was hot enough to violate a lot of hospital rules, and Egan couldn't wait until she'd healed enough to haul her off to his bed.

"So, what are you doing for the rest of your life?" Jordan asked with her mouth still against his.

"Spending it with you, of course." And he went back to her for another kiss.

* * * * *

Get 4 FREE REWARDS!

We'll send you 2 FREE Books plus 2 FREE Mystery Gifts.

Harlequin® Romantic Suspense books feature heart-racing sensuality and the promise of a sweeping romance set against the backdrop of suspense.

FREE
Value Over
$20

Get 4 FREE REWARDS!

We'll send you 2 FREE Books plus 2 FREE Mystery Gifts.

Harlequin Presents® books feature a sensational and sophisticated world of international romance where sinfully tempting heroes ignite passion.

FREE
Value Over
$20

YES! Please send me 2 FREE Harlequin Presents® novels and my 2 FREE gifts (gifts are worth about $10 retail). After receiving them, if I don't wish to receive any more books, I can return the shipping statement marked "cancel." If I don't cancel, I will receive 6 brand-new novels every month and be billed just $4.55 each for the regular-print edition or $5.55 each for the larger-print edition in the U.S., or $5.49 each for the regular-print edition or $5.99 each for the larger-print edition in Canada. That's a savings of at least 11% off the cover price! It's quite a bargain! Shipping and handling is just 50¢ per book in the U.S. and 75¢ per book in Canada.* I understand that accepting the 2 free books and gifts places me under no obligation to buy anything. I can always return a shipment and cancel at any time. The free books and gifts are mine to keep no matter what I decide.

Choose one: ☐ **Harlequin Presents®**
Regular-Print
(106/306 HDN GMYX)

☐ **Harlequin Presents®**
Larger-Print
(176/376 HDN GMYX)

Name (please print)

Address   Apt. #

City   State/Province   Zip/Postal Code

Mail to the **Reader Service:**
IN U.S.A.: P.O. Box 1341, Buffalo, NY 14240-8531
IN CANADA: P.O. Box 603, Fort Erie, Ontario L2A 5X3

Want to try 2 free books from another series! Call 1-800-873-8635 or visit www.ReaderService.com.

---

*Terms and prices subject to change without notice. Prices do not include sales taxes, which will be charged (if applicable) based on your state or country of residence. Canadian residents will be charged applicable taxes. Offer not valid in Quebec. This offer is limited to one order per household. Books received may not be as shown. Not valid for current subscribers to Harlequin Presents books. All orders subject to approval. Credit or debit balances in a customer's account(s) may be offset by any other outstanding balance owed by or to the customer. Please allow 4 to 6 weeks for delivery. Offer available while quantities last.

Your Privacy—The Reader Service is committed to protecting your privacy. Our Privacy Policy is available online at www.ReaderService.com or upon request from the Reader Service. We make a portion of our mailing list available to reputable third parties that offer products we believe may interest you. If you prefer that we not exchange your name with third parties, or if you wish to clarify or modify your communication preferences, please visit us at www.ReaderService.com/consumerschoice or write to us at Reader Service Preference Service, P.O. Box 9062, Buffalo, NY 14240-9062. Include your complete name and address.

HP19R

Get 4 FREE REWARDS!

We'll send you 2 FREE Books plus 2 FREE Mystery Gifts.

FREE Value Over **$20**

Both the **Romance** and **Suspense** collections feature compelling novels written by many of today's best-selling authors.

YES! Please send me 2 FREE novels from the Essential Romance or Essential Suspense Collection and my 2 FREE gifts (gifts are worth about $10 retail). After receiving them, if I don't wish to receive any more books, I can return the shipping statement marked "cancel." If I don't cancel, I will receive 4 brand-new novels every month and be billed just $6.74 each in the U.S. or $7.24 each in Canada. That's a savings of at least 16% off the cover price. It's quite a bargain! Shipping and handling is just 50¢ per book in the U.S. and 75¢ per book in Canada.* I understand that accepting the 2 free books and gifts places me under no obligation to buy anything. I can always return a shipment and cancel at any time. The free books and gifts are mine to keep no matter what I decide.

Choose one: ☐ **Essential Romance** ☐ **Essential Suspense**
       (194/394 MDN GMY7)   (191/391 MDN GMY7)

Name (please print)

Address   Apt. #

City   State/Province   Zip/Postal Code

Mail to the **Reader Service:**
IN U.S.A.: P.O. Box 1341, Buffalo, NY 14240-8531
IN CANADA: P.O. Box 603, Fort Erie, Ontario L2A 5X3

Want to try 2 free books from another series? Call 1-800-873-8635 or visit www.ReaderService.com.

READERSERVICE.COM

Manage your account online!

- Review your order history
- Manage your payments
- Update your address

> *We've designed the*
> *Reader Service website*
> *just for you.*

Enjoy all the features!

- Discover new series available to you, and read excerpts from any series.
- Respond to mailings and special monthly offers.
- Browse the Bonus Bucks catalog and online-only exculsives.
- Share your feedback.

Visit us at:
ReaderService.com